THE ARBITERS

Brook Lenker

MILFORD HOUSE

an imprint of Sunbury Press, Inc.
Mechanicsburg, PA USA

MILFORD HOUSE

an imprint of Sunbury Press, Inc.
Mechanicsburg, PA USA

For information about special discounts for bulk purchases, please contact Sunbury Press Orders Dept. at (855) 338-8359 or orders@sunburypress.com.

To request one of our authors for speaking engagements or book signings, please contact Sunbury Press Publicity Dept. at publicity@sunburypress.com.

FIRST MILFORD HOUSE PRESS EDITION: December 2024

Set in Adobe Garamond Pro | Interior design by Crystal Devine | Cover by Lawrence Knorr | Edited by Madelyn DeMatt.

Publisher's Cataloging-in-Publication Data
Names: Lenker, Brook, author.
Title: The arbiters / Brook Lenker.
Description: First trade paperback edition. | Mechanicsburg, PA : Milford House Press, 2024.
Summary: When a dam project threatens to flood their favorite haunts, Reily Watters and his friends fight back with their own form of 1970's justice. In this coming of age story, an adventuresome coed crew, and enterprising dog, discover love, acceptance, and the importance of taking a stand to protect planet earth.
Identifiers: ISBN : 979-8-88819-256-6 (paperback).
Subjects: YOUNG ADULT FICTION / Action & Adventure / General | YOUNG ADULT FICTION / Science & Nature / Environment | YOUNG ADULT FICTION / Social Themes / Activism & Social Justice | FICTION / Coming of Age | FICTION / Literary.

Designed in the USA
0 1 1 2 3 5 8 13 21 34 55

For the Love of Books!

In memory of the
Reverend Dr. Richard Lee Dowhower,
alpha of spirit,
lion of grace,
fountain of wisdom,
master of books

Acknowledgments

A big thank you to Lawrence Knorr, Madelyn DeMatt, and other staff at Sunbury Press for making this book a reality. I am also indebted to my beta readers–Andy Golba, Autumn Sabo, Ben Cramer, Charlie Young, Deidre Lenker, Margot Golba, Mike Youse, and Ray Solinski–for their critical eye and helpful suggestions. Thanks, too, to Demi Stevens for her editorial support and advice. The ongoing encouragement of friends and family energizes my writing, as does the love and support of my extraordinary wife and daughters. I am so appreciative.

1

Mannequin Creek coursed alongside Reily Watters, beautiful and mysterious, playful yet demure. Deep pools and cut banks transformed and delivered, archiving the boundless days. Scenes conveyed a comforting permanence—eternity as it ought to be—but things were changing. The carefree days of adolescence were numbered.

Would his favorite stream expire, too?

Air, thick and resinous, rested beneath the feathered tips of hemlocks, where water chanted without end. The soothing cadence, and blessed thoughts of a precocious girl, relaxed his dour mood.

For thousands of acres spanning north and south, the protected lands unfurled—a vast green blanket, crumpled and beloved. According to his father, Lenape and other indigenous peoples had lived and hunted in this part of eastern Pennsylvania for millennia before white settlers made a mess of things. Rumor had it the area contained their burial sites, too. Reily felt native during frequent explorations, though his ancestors came from Germany and Wales in the less distant past.

The muscular arch of a sycamore flagged his destination. Reily's best friend, Wil, crept closer and set his backpack on the bank.

"Hand me a fat one. There's a brownie down there."

Reily obliged. Wil, the master, went to work on a terminal mission of threading the hook through an earthworm.

Wil, a grade behind, doubled as a younger brother. As they were physically similar and nearly inseparable, Reily's father called them Siamese friends. When one of them had a family obligation that disrupted planned adventures, Reily was restless and awry.

Three casts later, Wil's line bounced as if an underwater kite fluttered on its end. He coaxed his prey to the shallows like a pied piper and landed a fine catch—red, orange, and white dappled on lubricated metal. Wil admired the living art. "Top notch, isn't she?" The troller extraordinaire extracted the hook with surgical care, liberating the trout to secret lairs. The ritual repeated.

The Mannequin treated its devotees to these and other pleasures. The area had the makings of a private preserve; intrusion was uncommon except for the serious angler. A hot day might entice other kids to venture a swim, but routine occupancy belonged to Reily and his trustees—pioneers on their own frontier.

"I'm eating." Reily dug into a musty bag for a bologna sandwich. "All I had this morning was a bowl of stale cornflakes."

The duffel had known better times. It belonged to his grandfather, a geologist, whose tales of rocks, mines, and snakes captivated Reily's young mind. *Never get yourself in a pit you can't get out of,* he would say with a slight laugh and a lecturing, arthritic finger. Grandad died two years earlier, but the bag still oozed his inquisitive spirit.

They sat on a log while eating their sandwiches. Wil passed him a bottle filled with fluorescent liquid—the gritty Tang was refreshing. "Do you think Colleen will come looking for us?"

Wil motioned for him to return the beverage. "Fifty-fifty chance." He spoke with indifference, the way he always did.

Known for roaming the neighborhood, Colleen Mills lived less than a mile from where the two currently sat. Tomboy tough with Wonder Woman eyes, she toyed with the hearts of many a guy.

Reily exhaled. *Don't be another chump in the chain.* But her sly smile couldn't escape his thoughts. He and his posse had one-track minds—except for fishing, of course. Only the prospect of a wily salmonid quelled quixotic longings.

"When I saw her at Dinardo's yesterday and told her we were coming down here, she said, and I quote, 'It would be fun to hang out with you and Wil.'"

Wil shrugged. "Okay, I'll change the odds to sixty-forty, but don't get your hopes up."

Despite one less year of life and one and a half fewer inches of height, Wil had mountains of wisdom and a chill vibe, cooler than a mountain creek. He also had his so-called "Say of the Day," a highfalutin one-word summary for the situation or emotion at hand. Compared to Wil and his weird linguistic habits, Reily saw himself as more excitable, but simultaneously relaxed, or as his mother said, distracted.

He focused on the water at his feet. It issued a reminder.

"Hey, we have to move up to the loch," Reily said, referring to the preeminent swimming spot always worth the walk. "But if we head there, do you think Colleen will find us?"

Wil stood and hoisted his pack. "You're hopeless, Watters. Hopeless."

Wednesday seemed like Saturday. The July day could have been any day, June through August. The freedom of wandering erased conventional measures of time, yet slow days along the Mannequin passed much too fast. There were less than fifty days before the start of the school year, when Reily and Wil would separate. High school would be a new planet without his friend.

Wil moved beside him, their paces almost in sync. "I saw a story in the paper this week that said our area is being considered for a lake and a dam that would make electricity. I wonder where they want to build it?"

"Probably the river," Reily said. "It already has a bunch of dams."

The overhead sun revealed the rounded cobbles on the bottom of the oblong pool, named for a more famous Scottish loch. That one contained a legendary monster, this one a formidable water snake. Reily beat Wil into the bracing water—respite within the secret wilds. Every summer they came here. God willing, they would be back for many more.

They swam for an hour in the visceral present, but Colleen, universal constant of Reily's dreams, upheld a gnawing absence.

2

Few fifteen-year-olds came any beefier than "Big Eddie" Knisely. With a chest as round as a trash can and sun-bleached hair that fell over a face unable to disguise its mischief, unpredictable should have been his middle name. He savored his crass reputation, but secretly yearned for the attention of the civilized objects in Reily's life—foremost, his far-out sister, Rachel, and their groovy mom, Karen.

Past the tree line, Kemp's field unfolded, hay and thistle shimmering in the heat. Next came the Watters's small farm, the edge of the suburbs and outfitting depot for all things outdoors. The house once anchored a 200-acre dairy. Eleven shrunken acres remained, gateway to many adventures with trees to climb, gardens to plunder, and hideaways for whatever purpose necessary.

Reily ambushed him at the front door. "I thought you were coming an hour ago?"

Eddie ignored the question. "What's up, Jethro? Are you losing weight?" Eddie knew Reily hated it when he called everyone Jethro like they were some redneck character out of the *Beverly Hillbillies*. But he loved to irritate Reily. "You know what I have in here?" Liquid sloshed in a coffee can with a plastic lid. "Smell it."

Reily did as directed, opening the top for a whiff. "*Phew*," he huffed, reeling from the harsh vapor.

Eddie wiggled his eyebrows. "Jack Daniels. The good stuff."

"You stole this from your pop?"

"Borrowed it."

Reily laughed. "I don't want to think about how you intend to return it."

They leaned against the rough, sawn boards on the west side of the Watters's barn. Eddie glanced around. "Where's your hot sibling?"

"Rachel and Mom went on college visits to Philadelphia. Dad's at a base in Florida. The ladies won't be back until evening."

Eddie put his face into the can and inhaled for dramatic effect before pouring the whisky into his gaping mouth, swallowing hard. "Tasty."

"You're messed up. I'll have a little, that's all." Reily sipped once, and then endured a bigger swig. "Boy, that's harsh."

"Don't be a pussy." Eddie took the can and drank again.

"You keep doing that and you'll be barfing before dinner," Reily recalled from the last time Eddie had "borrowed" booze. "I had to throw away my shoes."

A few hours at the Trexler-Lehigh County Game Preserve the year prior had Eddie slobbering over a girl from Schnecksville. He bought her a soda and a hot dog, but when he called her the the next day, she mentioned a boyfriend through her involvement with the Future Farmers of America. Eddie damned the FFA and tried using alchohol to wash away the disappointment. Reily's attempts at comfort had instead earned him the partially digested contents of Eddie's stomach.

"That was a one-time thing," Eddie defended. "I'll be fine, but you better have some more. We have hours to kill."

Reily indulged a few wimpy slurps. The two of them were slumped further along the barn wall, immobile.

Eddie tapped the last contents from the can and dropped it. "Let's go fishing."

"Did you bring your rod?"

"No, but I know you have an extra." He always used Reily's stuff and seldom gave it back. "Let's go to the pond . . . for a largemouth or two."

"Wil and I were there last week. All we caught were sunnies."

Eddie returned to his feet. "You have to know how to catch them."

From Reily's bedroom closet, Eddie grabbed a rod with a spinning reel and broken tip. Reily extracted an ultralight setup—a Christmas present from his father. Eddie couldn't remember the last time his own pop had gotten him anything of similar value or utility.

Eddie held a transistor radio at his ear, rocking his head to AM tunes as he led the way to the pond. Storm clouds loitered on the western horizon; asphalt simmered. Muggy air glued his t-shirt to his body, causing him to sweat like a pig at the Allentown Fair.

Reily hummed along to a refrain. "Who sings this?"

"Pure Prairie League."

"Cool song. Have you heard Bowie's new one?"

"My old man says he's a homo."

"I don't know, but who cares. It's a worthy song."

The radio crackled. Eddie craned his neck and stared at the Kemp Farm down the road. "Think they'll let us fish?"

"They have one of my mother's paintings. If Mrs. Kemp comes out, I'll reintroduce myself."

"Dad says she's half-crazy."

"Last year, she gave me a piece of homemade shoofly pie," Reily said. "She's alright."

They slipped past the white farmhouse and along the edge of a field with corn already three feet tall. A mowed path through alfalfa grass took them to the circular pond—an angler's Garden of Eden. Milfoil laced the shallows; velvet cattails guarded the opposite end. A metallic dragonfly whizzed between them.

Eddie clipped a bobber twenty inches above a weighted hook disguised with a refrigerated worm, courtesy of Reily. He cast toward the right corner, the red and white plastic ball sending ripples in all directions. "I'm trying my luck on the steeper side." After a series of tugs on the end of the line, he reeled in an empty hook.

"Don't take it personally," Reily spoke toward the pond as if advising the water striders. "Set the bobber six inches deeper and see if you can drop it center, in front of the cattails." Reily had yet to take a single cast.

Eddie followed the unneeded instructions. After a delicate splash, the only sound came from a distant cicada buzzing off-key on a favorite twig. They waited. Without warning, the bobber went under and the fiberglass rod bowed to the surface. Excitement coursed through Eddie. His arms and lips tightened as he attempted to haul in a substantial fish. It cooperated for a moment, before veering hard left. It shook twice. The line fell slack.

"Damn, that was a nice one." Eddie put the rod aside and lay back in the grass, closing his eyes. "I must have hooked his lip."

"I'll take a turn." Reily cast to the far side of the pond and retrieved the line at a slow, steady rate. The sequence repeated a dozen times. Thrashing and commotion brought Eddie back to life. The thin monofilament and nimble action of Reily's setup made every fish seem like a tarpon. A two-pound monster from the abyss of Kemp's pond became the great white in the new movie *Jaws*.

Reily held up the catch for inspection. "She's a bright one. Check out the orange by her pectoral fin. Sharp spines, too."

Eddie rubbed his eyes. "Nice bluegill. You should kill it."

"Why?"

"They're trash fish. They overpopulate the pond."

"That's ridiculous." Reily squatted and lowered the sunfish back in the water. "I think it swallowed the hook."

"Excellent, we can proceed with the killing." Eddie held an unhealthy interest in such things.

Reily worked needle-nosed pliers and managed to clip the line within the gasping mouth. "There. Enjoy the rest of your time." The fish shot away out of sight, life expectancy unknown.

Eddie frowned. "You're no fun, Watters."

"You're a sick dude."

They fished for half an hour with no further luck.

Eddie stepped away from the pond and peed.

"You want to go back to my house and get something to eat?" Reily asked.

Eddie zipped his shorts. "I'm more interested in nourishment for the mind. Pack up and follow me."

"I'm starving. This better be good."

A "For Sale" sign at the end of the Kemp's driveway pierced the sacred ground. It listed a local realtor.

"I wonder why they're selling." Reily sounded distraught.

"Probably too much for the old geezers to care for."

Eddie hiked the fence line between the Kemps's lower acreage and an old Christmas tree farm with pines too big and shabby for holiday use. The back of the land bordered the flat part of the Mannequin's woodlands, a quarter-mile wide. His oversized sneakers swished through the leaf litter until he stopped at an enormous tree, seven feet across at the base.

Reily gawked upwards. "It's a white oak. I can tell by the rounded margins of the leaves."

"Two years in the scouts taught you something."

"It's an impressive tree, but somehow I know this isn't why we're here."

Eddie pinched his eyes. "You are a smart one, Reily-san. Very perceptive. I teach you well." He loved to channel allusions of *Kung Fu*, his favorite TV show.

"So what's the surprise?"

Eddie guided Reily around the back of the tree to a gaping cavity at ground level. "Reach in there."

Reily got on his knees to see into the crevice. He slid in his arm and pulled out a dark green trash bag. Inside was a trove of magazines, the pages glossy, the contents dirty and forbidden.

The bare-busted image of Miss June 1974 turned Reily's cheeks pink. "Where did you get these?"

Eddie winked. "Older brothers, they're the best."

"They gave these to you?"

Eddie sat down against the tree. "Hell no. I took them."

"Wil should see these."

"Don't tell him. He'll steal them."

Hunched over, Reily leafed through one issue then another, pausing as sights warranted.

Eddie drooled over his own serving of sultry women. A low rumble diverted his attention. A darkening sky. "We better go, Jethro. Man, my stomach doesn't feel right."

Reily fed the viewed material into the bag Eddie held open. "You shouldn't have drunk so much."

Eddie squatted to secure the pornography. He felt gloomy, as if the pinup girls were breaking up with him. He stood up and sensed a greater discomfort—a sickening heave followed.

"Oh no." Reily dodged the lumpy splatter.

"Oh yes." Eddie wiped his mouth with the back of his hand and smiled. "I feel better already."

Reily shook his head. "You're a psycho."

Light flickered. God had wiggled a wall switch. Artillery followed. They ran with their fishing gear beneath the turbocharged heavens. By the Kemp Farm, a billion liquid bullets came out of the slate above. Eddie hustled through the deluge, Reily at his back.

Huffing and puffing, they drip-dried on the Watters's porch. Without asking permission, Eddie entered the house and rooted through the refrigerator. "Mind if I have a Coke? Is that chicken salad?"

"Help yourself." Reily poured a glass of ice water. "I'm dying of thirst."

After Eddie had his fill and the storm retreated, he gave Reily a high-five and sauntered away to the mutterings of speckled hens. Golden rays drenched the Watters's barn and outbuildings in disorganized colors—a scene beckoning capture. Eddie hadn't used his paints and brushes since winter. *What a waste of time*, his old man had laughed. Eddie could still hear the jaded words. But Reily and Wil complimented his watercolors, and a girl in his art class had called him "amazing." Reily's mother said he was "a natural talent." Tough guys could paint, too.

A dull ache grew in his temples. No more whisky. However, he had zero intention to give up painting, no matter what his father thought.

3

Through prescription bifocals, Merle Darkes leafed through engineering descriptions while his elderly mother dueled with the prosthodontist in a private room. Over the rim of his glasses, he noted a rack of children's books in the humdrum waiting room. The cover of *Winnie-the-Pooh* resuscitated buried memories of the singular time his father read to him. His droning monologue made Eeyore, by comparison, an eternal optimist. Only his philandering father could steal magic from the hundred-acre wood. Merle hoped to create his own form of father-free magic from a few thousand acres more.

Merle's new dam project, absent Tiggers and Piglets, dripped with honey—pending the accuracy of initial estimates. Names like Fort Peck and Oroville came to mind, water racing through spillways honed with curvilinear precision. Energy giants *and* tourist meccas. Pleasure and power *could* mix.

At age seven, the roaring rage of Niagara Falls scoured a special place in Merle's rudimentary heart. While most boys dickered with BB guns, baseball cards, or Matchbox cars, he dallied in the dirt, constructing miniature manifestations of land transformation. Earthen neighborhoods sprouted where a sandbox disintegrated, and little lakes took shape like planned Florida subdivisions. He terraced the watered creations, and connected them with straws—his earliest work on pipelines.

Merle, the nascent hydrophilic engineer and entrepreneur, had a harrowing setback as a prepubescent teen. An amusement park flume ride dropped several terrifying stories, and upon impact, unleashed a tsunami, inundating the pseudo watercraft. The event instilled a permanent fear of falling, and—for a period of years—outright hydrophobia. Counseling later detangled the raw feelings. A mathematical revelation at college solved the riddle of the tidal wave in a complex calculation factoring volume, angle, speed, and displacement.

Mother's agitated voice disturbed his ruminations, as it had on too many occasions to count. The doctor, or an aid, moderated her disruption beneath the agonizing trill of a drill. His attention returned to the engineering report and kinetic projections. Numbers and details consoled.

The new project site tendered optimum features. Room aplenty. An industrial legacy. Proximity to customers. A lifespan lease at meager cost.

Merle sensed eyes upon him. The do-good Ranger Rick raccoon peered from the bookrack, stuck to the cover of the nature magazine, indoctrinating the nation's youth to the fad of conservation. The dogma spelled danger to doers like him. A country incessantly stalled. Advancement be damned.

4

Ceaseless ringing. Reily reached across his bed and hit the top right button, ending the rude noise. He sat up to collect his thoughts. Monday. Forty-five minutes to get to practice.

Someone held a newspaper at the kitchen table. The time of day, the cup of black coffee, and slice of toast slathered with blackberry jam certified the hominid as Reily's dad, Keith Watters.

His father lowered the classifieds. "Swimming starts today?"

Reily cleared his sleepy throat. "Yeah, it feels like it just ended."

"Welcome to real life, the regular grind. You get used to it." Advice from a man who was always punctual, never ruffled, and consistently gracious.

From the pantry, Reily rummaged a pack of strawberry pop-tarts. His dad got up and poured him a glass of orange juice before refilling his own coffee cup from a metal percolator. Reily sat down opposite him.

"Are you shopping for something?" Reily nodded toward the newspaper.

"I wanted to see if there were any mowers. Ours is fading, I'm afraid. It's using too much oil."

His father always worried about such things. The bearing in the clothes dryer made a funny noise. The furnace had an uncharacteristic odor. A mechanical disaster lay waiting. "Are there real estate ads in that section?"

His father, lean and neatly groomed as ever, looked at him with surprise. "Are you planning to move out?"

Reily laughed, ejecting pastry crumbs. "No, but I saw a 'For Sale' sign at the Kemps' house." The notion of the place changing hands bothered him. Was someone dying? Were they out of money?

His father sat back in the chair and folded his hands on top of his head. "Margaret has a bad heart, I believe. I ran into Russell at Sears a few weeks ago. He said she wasn't doing well."

Reily stared back. Was his dad telepathic? "Do you think that's why they're selling?"

"Maybe. I'll see what I can find out." His father tapped his watch. "You better get moving."

Reily finished his juice. "Who would buy it? Another farmer?"

His father folded the sports section. "Doubtful. I would guess a developer. You can fit a lot of houses on all that space."

"That would be awful. We use the pond. The fields are the shortcut to the creek." A tide of indignation rose within. "We'd have to stop them."

His father shook his head and frowned. "You'll have to learn that things don't always go the way you want them to. A developer has a right to build houses. There's not much you can do about that."

Reily stood from the table and took his plate to the sink, envisioning a bulldozer ravaging the Kemp place.

Outside, a rosy mist arose from the fields, harbinger of heat to come. He mounted his ten-speed, the tape on the handlebars unraveling, the handgrips torn. Before long, he would borrow a car from Mom or Dad, a driver's license in his pocket. The premise sounded fun, but what would life be like without pedaling? He loved the wind in his face.

School and the pool were three miles and four turns from home. If he hit the single traffic light on green, he could make it in thirteen minutes. He felt sluggish this morning, entering the door to the natatorium at the eighteen-minute mark. The humid interior held the routine reek of chlorine. Tiled mosaics contained three kinds of squares: surf blue, blanched gray, and sadly chipped. Some faces were familiar, others obscure. High school swim camp disqualified ninth graders like Wil. It would be strange to swim without him.

Papers were distributed. A speech commenced. The new head coach wore a t-shirt failing to hide a beer belly, and when he called himself Mr. Finn, Reily struggled to refrain from laughing.

"For the next four weeks, I want you to dream about water. Think of yourselves as fish, my fry and fingerlings, navigating a swift river but able to move upstream because you are tireless and tenacious. I'll challenge you, but in the end, you will be better." Mr. Finn spoke of swimming like the Presbyterian pastor spoke of God, only he wore a polished whistle draped around his neck, not a tarnished crucifix.

Introductions followed with each participant stating their name and competitive swimming dossier. A black kid, the only black kid and as dark as the pipe on the wood burning stove at home, looked lost as he stood against the wall. With a distinct accent, the boy introduced himself as Ben Kabumba. Ben had never raced before.

Reily ended up sharing a lane with Ben for a relay workout. During a five-minute break, the boy opened up to him.

"We came here in May from Uganda to get away from Idi Amin. He did terrible things in our country. My parents hope the United States will give us a new start." Ben seemed earnest and easy to like.

"Will you be in tenth grade here at West Bethlehem?"

"Yes, but I should be in eleventh grade because I am already sixteen years old."

Reily took a sip of water from a Styrofoam cup. "That will make it easier for you. How do you say your last name?"

"Ka-boom-ba." Ben emphasized the middle sound. "My friends in Kampala, the city where we lived, called me Boom."

"So should I use Ben or Boom?"

Ben flashed a big smile with teeth as bright as ivory. "I leave it up to you, Reily." He had already mastered the pronunciation.

On the way home, Reily detoured to Wil's house. The brick Cape Cod on Delaware Street matched all the others, except a covered boat occupied the front yard and a trailer sat in back. Reily leaned the bike beside the garage and rapped on the front door. No one answered. He jiggled the handle and let himself in. The house carried a constant odor—a mixture of motor oil and sugar cookies. Wil's dad ran the service department at the Ford dealership; his mother managed the bakery at the grocery store. Their occupations were also pastimes. Mr. Wisnoski lived under his own automobile, his shirts ever streaked with grease. Any occasion became the perfect occasion for Mrs. Wiz to whip up a sheet cake or a batch of sticky buns. The extra calories influenced her physique, but the kitchen guaranteed a larder of sweets. Reily wondered what kinds awaited him this day, but first, he crept up the stairs to Wil's room.

Feet protruded from beneath a navy blue sheet decorated with anchors. A pillow half-covered Wil's head. Breaths whistled from his friend's nose.

Reily jostled the bed. "Seize the day, Rip Van Winkle."

Wil startled and squinted, averse to light streaming through the curtains. "What time is it?"

"Nine-thirty."

"What? Why'd you get me up so early?"

"I was on my way back from swimming and I have to tell you . . . the girls got 'well developed' this summer."

Wil sat up, perkier. "Well developed, huh? Man, I'll miss swimming with all of you this year."

"The year will go fast, don't worry. Did your dad leave any coffee? Get dressed so we can strategize about Colleen. I need your counsel."

Wil flopped back and slammed a pillow over his face. "Give it up, Watters. You're obsessed."

Reily ignored the muffled comment and trudged downstairs. Black syrup remained in the pot. He retrieved a mug from a hook and poured tar, diluting it with powdered creamer. As hoped, a cherry strudel sat on the counter. He tore a piece off and stuffed it in his mouth, chewing to the creak of Wil's footsteps.

"I can't believe you drink that." Wil pointed his squared chin at the cup of coffee. "You'll probably start smoking next. They go together." He stood at the entrance to the kitchen, his hair matted, a white gob of toothpaste at the corner of his mouth.

Wil's father never had coffee in one hand without a cigarette in the other—except indoors. He could balance both and simultaneously perform any task. Reily took an oversized swallow from the coffee mug to annoy Wil. In those few moments upstairs, his friend managed to brush his teeth and outfit himself in jeans, sneakers, and a 76ers t-shirt. In spite of other deficiencies, Wil properly prioritized a day's activities over painstaking hygiene.

Wil prepped a bowl of Cheerios and sat down next to him on the other stool of the breakfast nook. A window afforded views of backyards and backsides of houses. Reily counted two swingsets, one above ground pool, and a clothesline free of lacy underthings this weekday morning.

On lucky days, Wil's divorced neighbor—barely old enough for marriage and home ownership—pinned her bras and other tantalizing garments for display. Bras made Reily think of Colleen.

"Should I call her?"

"Who?" Wil spit milk with the question.

"Colleen."

"You need to see a psychiatrist."

"No, I just need to see her eyes . . . they're as blue as the ocean."

"Then do it. I'm sick of hearing her name."

"I don't have her number."

"The phone book is on the shelf under the phone. Her mom's name is Vicki Mills."

Reily almost choked on coffee. "How'd you know that?"

"She's in bridge club with my mom, but she never comes."

Reily feigned exasperation. "And you never told me."

"For your own good."

Time for action—before courage crumbled. In the tiny text of the white pages, he located a Vicki Mills. The street matched Colleen's last known whereabouts.

Wil gestured at the phone with his head, the Wisnoski method of encouragement.

Reily picked up and dialed, growing nervous with every ring.

5

"How was synchronized swimming?" Wil chuckled at his own sarcasm. How could Reily endure early morning practices and recurring ear infections? Anymore, chlorinated workouts had zero appeal, but, in an uncommon gesture of semi-solidarity, Wil began his day on the early side, and met Reily at the Watters's house minutes after his best friend rolled in from another aquatic torture session.

"Very funny." Reily opened antique cupboards in search of food. "Sometimes I think my parents have an aversion to groceries."

"Go easy on them. Your dad's always away and your mom . . . well, paintings take a lot of time."

"Yeah, but if they want me to help take care of things around here, they have to feed me. I'm starving."

"Let's go to Dinardo's. They have their sub special on Wednesdays. Top-notch." Wil had his mind set on a twelve-inch cheesesteak. "From there, we can head to the park for hoops."

"To kick my butt again." Reily pointed to Wil's new basketball. "I'll let you reign on the court, but don't even try to stay with me in the 100-meter breaststroke."

"Go change your damn clothes, Mark Spitz. There are other breasts I'd like to stroke. The *Say of the Day* is possibility."

On the bike ride to town, Reily rambled about his breakthrough with Colleen, his dad's upcoming trip to a base in Germany, and his new friend on the swim team—a Ugandan kid with an explosive nickname. Reily exuded subtle enthusiasm for everything—a slug encounter, the sound of a cricket, the pattern of a jet's contrail. He babbled like a brook, when in a certain mindset.

Dinardo's buzzed with business, the sandwiches as mouthwatering as ever. Gooey provolone hung from the remains of a roll. Fragments of greasy meat and caramelized onion spattered the plate. Fizzy, fragrant root beer washed down the final bite while across a small, unbalanced table, Reily chewed on a meatball sub in self-absorbed delight.

Wil crunched the last bits of ice in his cup. "Where are you taking your bombshell on your Friday foray?"

"Luckenbach Falls. The back trail. The trudge along the creek is pretty tough . . . I don't want to scare her off prematurely."

"You better pace yourself or other things may happen prematurely."

Reily stabbed him in the arm with a straw. "Seriously, a sprained ankle would make for a crummy first date."

"And so might your hair. You're starting to resemble Todd Rundgren."

A second straw stab missed its mark. "Yours isn't far behind, Engle-bert Humperdinck. Pretty soon you'll have sideburns."

Wil volleyed more celebrity comparisons as they left the restaurant. On the hilltop, an old man walked his collie through the verdant grass of Weyant Park. The courts called—empty and recently re-lined.

Wil sank consecutive shots from the free throw line. Reily hit one out of five. Watters had the sturdiness of a ship, but the coordination of a drunken sailor.

"Okay, let's do one-on-one to ten. Half court."

Reily got lucky on a fade from the baseline, but Wil took charge thereafter, even showing off a pair of left side lay-ups over Reily's out-stretched limbs.

Reily rested on a bench, perspiration beading down his chest. "You're quick, but I can't believe I'm letting a junior high kid beat me. Next time, I'll try harder."

"Screw off, brother. I'll be on the high school team by this time next year."

"Nope." Reily smirked. "Because tryouts aren't until the fall."

Wil flung the basketball at his friend's head.

Reily closed his eyes. "The sphere of orange shall do me no harm, but the bright blue globe, that we call home, wants us to disarm and join arms for the brotherhood of good."

Wil suppressed a laugh. "Are you on drugs? Is Eddie introducing you to wacky weed? I wouldn't put it past him."

"I'm attempting poetry. I figure I have to impress Colleen somehow."

"You say stuff like that and she'll think you've been eating shrooms."

"Speaking of Eddie, did I tell you about the magazines?"

"What magazines? The naked kind?"

Reily nodded. "He has a secret stockpile in the woods."

Wil faked a frown. "I can't believe he didn't share."

"Was that a stack of *Time* magazines I saw next to your bed yesterday?"

Wil straightened. "You have a problem with current events?"

"Just teasing. I figured they contained scantily-clad sunbathing beauties or other stimulating content."

Wil scratched his head. "Don't tell anyone. This is for your ears only. I think I want to be a writer someday." An idea, initially vague and brief, had become firmly engrained.

"For X-rated movies, I bet."

"No, I mean it." He parked himself beside Reily. "I get pulled into the articles I read. I want to write like that."

"News stories, investigations . . . those kinds of things?"

"Yeah, I think so. Certainly not poetry." Wil gave a sly elbow to his friend.

Reily leaned back, placing his hands behind his head. "You'd be great at it. You have the snarky edge of a writer. I wish I knew what I wanted to do."

Wil recovered the ball and began to dribble on the macadam. "Just don't plan on playing in the NBA."

Reily chased him before play resumed. Another round to ten. Tied at three each, Reily used his slight height advantage to block a shot and make a rare, nimble move to score and take the lead. Wil had enough, and finessed the ball around Reily. As he launched toward the rim, Reily's lanky leg caught his shin, catapulting him forward, introducing his forehead to the steel pole with a rude smack.

When Wil emerged into consciousness, a voice spoke near his face. He could not see the voice, but he knew it belonged to Reily. *Why was it pitch black?* "Are my eyes open?" He could barely formulate words.

"Are you okay? You hit your head hard."

"I can't see."

"You're probably just dizzy."

"No, I really can't see anything." Wil fought tears.

Reily gripped his shoulder. "Take a deep breath and close your eyes, then try again."

Wil followed the instructions and counted to three in a slow tempo. He concentrated on the unclenching of his eyelids. A nauseating shower of light rewarded him. "Hey, they're working, but I think I'm going to be sick."

"Take it easy. You need to see a doctor. I'll get to a phone and call your folks."

Wil suppressed the urge to vomit. "How did you do that?"

"What?"

"Restored my sight."

"I didn't do anything."

Wil smiled in delirium. "Divine intervention. You must have been paying attention in Sunday school." The sun formed a halo around Reily's tipped head.

"You're nonsensical."

"It's going to be my first published article—'The Miracle of Reily Watters.'"

6

Merle netted a dead frog from the pristine surface of his vinyl-lined pool. He catapulted the limp amphibian over the cedar-slatted privacy fence into the neglected backyard of an ailing neighbor. On Sunday mornings, swimming, in his distinctive, tadpole style, substituted for religion as a pure and cleansing rite, but the frogs had invaded like slimy locusts—a possible sign of a disgruntled deity.

With a sweetened cup of coffee an arm's reach away, he adjusted his flaccid flanks on a deck chair and resumed review of the preliminary application to federal regulators. Each section required an exhaustive scouring for errors. The national budget might have more brevity. One oversight could cost him time and money—commodities too precious to waste.

The environmental subsections, bereft copious detail, contained a menu of boxes checked with suspect rigor. Deficiencies could drag things out until funding evaporated. One endangered species or water supply concern could terminate any momentum. He heated within—his scalp, unprotected by thinning shocks, was scorching in the merciless sun. Sunscreen failed to soothe multiplying misgivings. *Maybe I should invest in Elliot Berman's solar technologies.* It had to bring less aggravation and greater recompense.

Water authority lands spanned more than 3,200 acres of the Upper Mannequin watershed. Eastern Power wanted half of it for the pumped storage reservoir. This would be his second such project as CEO. The first repurposed lands decimated by strip mining. Straight forward. A win for every side. This one would require clear-cutting a mature forest and enduring the whining of people oblivious to the economic benefits of abundant electricity.

Merle rose to enter the pool and placed a folded towel upon the concrete edge. Tepid water refreshed as he descended inlaid steps. He floated on his back, bobbing like a manatee, dreaming of lucrative pay-days should all things proceed expeditiously. A pasty splatter of white goo landed on his exposed stomach and trickled into his naval. The thrashing that ensued mimicked the breaching behavior of a humpback whale. To his chagrin, the excrement disbursed throughout the disinfected aqueous playground, while the culprit landed on the fence top. The mockingbird jested him with a searing, repetitious whistle.

Merle's exploits had won him few friends in the animal kingdom . . . or the human realm, for that matter.

7

Mr. Finn approached Reily's face. At close range, his coach's eyes seemed too far apart, as if they were migrating to the sides of his head, like a flounder in reverse.

"Watters, you can't let up. Push that six-foot skeleton of yours until nothing's left. What's going on?"

"Sorry coach, I'll work harder." Reily dropped his head and noticed a puddle forming at his own gangly feet. "May I get my towel?"

"No," Finn glared. "Get back in the water. Ten more laps."

"Yes, sir." The other kids were on water break and saw the exchange. Reily became self-conscious, either due to the coach's words or an inspiring gawk from Cindy Sutherland—a pretty, older girl on the team. He returned to his lane and began to churn.

The rhythm of his strokes induced tranquility, a state magnified by multiple phone conversations with Colleen Mills in a stretch of four days and the mellow elation of knowing they were meeting in two hours to go for a hike.

Reily finished the bonus workout, dried his torso, and took a spot at the end of the bench. Coach lectured the group about entries and flip turns. The voice drifted. Colleen's visage reappeared.

"You must always be determined. It's about leadership, being a role model. Right, Reily?" Mr. Finn glowered with his hands on his hips.

"Yes . . . always." Caught. Again.

Coach exhaled and refocused his attention to the team. "Now, I want you all to put on fins and do twenty-five laps of crawl stroke. When finished, you can go home. I'll see you again bright and early on Monday."

Ben Kabumba handed Reily a set of flippers. "Coach is watching you," he whispered in a bass tone laugh.

"I'll say. How did you do this morning?"

"Very well, I think . . . and I like it more every day." Boom stole a look toward Cindy Sutherland and flexed his eyes.

"I know what you mean." Reily watched her lithe, long arms stab the water. Such a graceful swimmer.

Twenty-five laps elapsed in a blur. Reily bee-lined to the locker room and prepped for Mission Colleen. He showered and sanitized with a splash of cologne, and stuffed wet items to the bottom of his canvas duffel beside a lunch packed for two. The zipper resounded, sealing the deal. The time had arrived.

Reily pedaled hard. To smother his anxiety, he thought of hiking. Was it the intrigue of exploring or the vitality of outdoor exercise he liked best? Nature taught and revealed. Trees were quiet friends—sage, supportive, and strong as steel. And why did he so desire Colleen? She could be dismissive and haughty, but beneath the tough, outer bark hid a soft, vulnerable layer. Most guys treated her poorly. Single-minded loggers cutting her down. He would be her arborist.

Colleen lived at the bottom of King Street, in a valley after a protracted rise. A ranch house with a weedy lawn and missing shutters bore the memorized street number. A side door opened and into the shadows of a shaded carport stepped Ms. Mills. The ponytail and denim shorts left him speechless.

"Do I need to bring anything?" Colleen spoke as she approached. In her indifferent tenor, Reily detected a smile.

"Just your bike." He didn't recognize his own voice. "I have lunch for us . . . and water."

"Great." She turned to retrieve her bike from the far wall. Her hair reached halfway down her short, but sensational, back.

In the sunlight, her eyes became luscious, magnetic sapphires. An image of the rock band Sweet conformed to the bosom of her t-shirt. He centered his racing mind on her forlorn bike. It lacked gears and tread. "I'll take the lead, just follow me. It's a few miles to the gate. We can hide our bikes there and hike in."

"Got it, but don't ride too fast. You're in better shape than I am."

He begged to differ.

"We're almost there." Reily pulled his bike to the side of the road. "Do you want some water?"

Colleen dismounted behind him. "Yeah, it's hot out here."

He handed her an aluminum canteen long without its G.I. Joe covering. She drank like a lost puppy. Water dripped down her chin and onto her shirt as she gulped.

"Thanks." She caught him staring at her neck. "I was thirsty."

"Do you ever go to the creek?" he transitioned abruptly.

Colleen bent down to tie her shoe. "Hardly. We don't go anywhere. My brother moved out in the spring and it's just my mom and me."

"What about your dad? I mean, where's he?"

She shrugged. "Who knows? Who cares? He divorced my mom when I was five. I don't even get birthday cards from him."

"I'm sorry." *Another humdinger of a response.*

Colleen exhaled a discouraged breath and jumped on her bike. "Don't be. My dad's a loser."

The road ended at a cul-de-sac where a yellow-painted padlocked gate marked the beginning of the trail, an abandoned road from long ago. They stashed the bikes behind a thicket of multi-flora rose and set off, Colleen walking beside him. He shortened his stride to match her pace. A belt of forest extended before them. Wil had told him it ran practically the whole way to the gap in Blue Mountain. Their footsteps spooked a deer that crashed through the underbrush and out of sight downhill. A pile of trash lay beside the trail. Rusted beer cans sparkled, peppered with broken glass. Car batteries leaked caustic ooze.

Colleen stopped. "That's gross." Her interjection shattered a void in the conversation.

Reily shook his head in disgust. "Someone's not doing their part to keep America beautiful."

Colleen pushed her hands in her pockets, eyes twinkling. "The Indian from the TV commercial is mad. He'll kick their butt if he finds them." Reily already liked her sly sense of humor.

The trail rose higher, past beech trees bearing carved messages and chestnut oaks better armored. Reily spied another species and showed

Colleen its three styles of leaves. "See, one's a mitten, one has three 'toes', and one looks normal. Sassafras is the only tree that does that." He hoped he didn't sound like a nerd.

She gazed at him. "And how do you know so much about nature?"

"I don't, really. I earned the Forestry merit badge in seventh grade and had to learn tree identification."

"I'm impressed, but let's keep going." Colleen took the lead, as if she knew the way.

Reily stumbled after her. "It's about another half mile to the upper falls. Wil and I usually hang out on the section of creek closer to my house, but sometimes we come up here. It's incredible." They were almost to the crest of the small ridge. The creek and falls occupied the valley on the other side. *Where should we picnic?*

"So you're friends with Wil Wisnoski?" Colleen asked over her shoulder.

"Yep, best friends." *Why did she want to know?* Every girl became smitten with Wil. "I've known him for years—through school, swimming, youth group, and . . ." A wooden stake with a tassel of pink ribbon caught his eye, then another in the distance. He pointed to the intrusion. "Wonder what that's for?"

"There's writing." Colleen got on her knees to read the words. Her shirt scrunched up, revealing the lower back convergence of a one-piece bathing suit. "It says Eastern Power, LLC."

"Strange." He counted three more stakes as they hiked downhill.

"I can hear the falls," Colleen said.

Before them, tucked behind a straight, soaring tulip poplar tree, water cascaded over ragged rock, dropping ten feet into a crystalline pool. A dry gravel bar made a beach, well-suited for outdoor dining.

Reily slipped the duffel off his back and retrieved two semi-mushed peanut butter and jelly sandwiches, handing one to Colleen. "Here's your gourmet lunch."

They fed without talking. Rushing headwaters made romantic background music—Mannequin jazz. Blackberry jam streaked the corner of Colleen's mouth. He rummaged in his bag for a napkin to no avail, but when he raised his frazzled head, Colleen had begun to disrobe.

"Can we swim in there?" She motioned to the water below the falls.

"Sort of. It's only four feet deep." Reily watched her kick the shorts off her now bare feet. The striped swimsuit exposed dreamy portions of a well-toned and tanned body. She dazzled. He felt out of body.

Colleen strode into the lair of frogs and fish and splashed Reily from afar. "Aren't you coming in?"

The chilly drops induced an inner warmth. Slippery-when-wet creatures never *previously* had this effect. An embarrassing, minimalistic racing swimsuit waited in his bag, but current clothing would suffice. He ripped off his sneakers before charging into the pool.

Colleen laughed and dripped, her hair shining like fresh blacktop. They inched closer to the tumbling water, seeing mini rainbows in the light mist. Colleen kept laughing. Jubilant jackal. Voluptuous vixen.

"Cool place, isn't it?" Reily said.

Colleen nodded and lowered herself to the bottom, her head remaining above the surface.

Reily took it as a cue and positioned himself beside her. Their backs were to the falls. Before them, the forest trees stood sentinel, protective of their ritual.

Colleen nibbled her lower lip, thinking too hard. She turned and peered up at him. "Thanks for bringing me here, Reily." She raised herself without warning, and planted a kiss.

It ended as quickly as it began—a moist and invigorating smack of sensory and neurological bliss. Colleen stood and clambered to the base of the vertical rock. "Where to next?"

Reily played along. "Wherever you want to go." Nothing less. He had morphed into an indentured subject, pleased to be of service on the best day of his life. The word *groovy* came to mind, the lingering sentiment after a delicious smooch from the most gorgeous girl in school.

8

Boom caught up with Reily leaving practice. Coach Finn shouted at all the swimmers, but disproportionately preferred to shout at his new friend.

"He should not have embarrassed you like that. You didn't deserve it."

Reily half-smiled. "Thanks, but I probably did. I feel tired today, but good. I got to see Colleen twice in the last three days."

Now Boom smiled. He always smiled. Sometimes the corners of his mouth hurt. "Very nice. She is your girlfriend?"

"I don't know. Maybe. That would be fine with me."

Boom tightened his backpack for the walk home. "Are you going to see her today?"

"Nope. Her mom said she has to paint her bedroom." Reily dropped his shoulders. "No Colleen today."

"We should do something. I am going crazy this summer. Besides swimming, there isn't much to do."

Reily removed his bike from the stand. "Well, what does Boom like to do?"

"Good question. People assume I enjoy basketball, because many black people play basketball, but I dislike it." Boom gestured with both hands, underscoring his disdain for the game. "I don't even know why."

"So, you're not a sports guy, except for swimming?"

"I run a lot . . . outside, not on a track, but I hate traffic and noise."

Reily nodded as if his head was loose. "I don't run much, but I hike. My friends and I love to fish, too. I live near the creek."

"Are there foot trails?" Boom pictured himself parallel to a lively river, deer-legged, but hushed as a fox. The outdoors made him forget the disruption of switching hemispheres and adjusting to life in America.

"Yes, some, but most of the time we bushwhack to wherever we want to go." Reily straddled his bike and rode in a tight circle. "Why don't we go back to my house? I'll show you the woods, firsthand. Consider it a guided tour."

Boom felt his cheeks reach for his eyes. "That would be wonderful."

Without a bike, Boom did his best to keep up, but when they finally arrived at Reily's house, the effort had been worth it. The shade of the porch cooled him after the long trek. Other buildings, mature and dissimilar, weathered on the property. Things had a timeworn quality. He imagined rich stories with every stone and board.

Reily motioned toward a distant field. "The woods are just on the other side. Let's find something to eat before we head down."

Boom followed him inside, letting his eyes explore the intricate art upon the walls and the labyrinth of doors and halls. Wooden floors appeared rustic, but well maintained. "Your house is . . . what do they say . . . historic?"

Reily paused in a giant kitchen. "This end of the house dates to 1885, although it's been remodeled by different owners. My grandfather bought the farm in 1925, but he had to sell off a slew of acres during the Depression."

Boom heard clomping feet. "Who is making that noise?"

Reily barely flinched. "Only one person has steps that heavy."

A burly kid burst through the front door. Boom recognized him, but didn't know his name. "What's up, Jethro?"

Reily jostled the newcomer. "Not much, big guy."

The kid shot Boom a blank gawp.

"Eddie, this is Boom. He's on the swim team with me."

"Oh," Eddie replied. "Got it."

Boom considered the cold response. Nothing new. Mean looks, hostile comments, and strange behaviors were a daily occurrence.

"We're going to the creek. You want to come?" Reily rocked on his feet, waiting for a reply. "Come on, Knisely."

The boy named Eddie chewed his lip. "I can't. My old man needs me to do a bunch of stuff. I was just stopping by."

"What are you up to tomorrow?" Reily implored Eddie in his encouraging way. "Wil needs visitors. He can't do anything for another week."

Eddie wore a sour face. "I don't know. I'll let you know." He stomped away and out the door without another word.

Boom turned to Reily, "Why did he call you Jethro? Is that a nickname?"

Reily smiled. "That's what he calls all of his friends."

Sunshine pulled them through parallel, infinite rows of corn, the stalks rivaling Boom in height. "Thank you for the sandwich," he said to Reily, who seemed preoccupied with navigation.

The crops ceased and the ground flattened. Evergreens sprouted along a rusty fence. Where metal wires sagged to meet untamed grasses, an odd tree arose, outfitted with pale red fruits and thin, sharp spikes.

Reily tapped his finger against one of them. "Be careful, they're little daggers."

"Interesting." Boom paused to examine the intricate, woody architecture. "Do you know what kind of tree this is?"

Reily closed his eyes for a moment, scouring for a memory. "Hawthorn, that's it. There's actually a bird that spears its prey against the needles."

"You know ecology very well. When we lived in Uganda, my father worked for the Game and Fisheries Department." Boom remembered with joy the rides in Father's Land Rover and the excitement at seeing animals in the bush.

"That's cool. Did you have lions there?"

Boom tested the thorns. "Yes, but they are not abundant like before. Poaching and loss of habitat have reduced their population."

Reily grimaced. "Nature loses out all the time."

Deer tracks tempted them into the forest. Gnats swirled around Boom's face in the humid understory. He recognized the pattern of a maple leaf, but other leaves were unfamiliar. The perfection of another tree sought his attention. He slid his hand along the smooth, buffed bark. "Do you know this one?"

"That's easy. American beech. I think of the beach and how the surf and sand wear stuff down."

"Good trick." Boom grinned. "Do you have books that teach about trees and plants?"

"A couple of different ones. You can borrow them if you'd like." Reily retrieved a branch off the ground. His rangy hair looked the part of mountain men Boom had seen in movies.

"That would be very nice. Ah, you like to hike with a stick?"

"Usually . . . I'm not sure why." Reily cupped a hand behind his ear. "Do you hear the creek?"

Boom leaned forward, harvesting enchanting sounds. "I think I do."

"This way." Reily tromped in a new direction.

Boom followed his footsteps. Life abounded with every step. A salamander squirmed for cover. A box turtle skulked in slow motion silence. A red-capped songbird searched for insects. Roving brought unlimited delight, but halted too soon. Reily had found his river.

Sparkling water tumbled across scattered rocks, speaking a jubilant language. Boom stated the first word that entered his mind. "Fantastic."

Reily studied the watercourse. "We could spend the rest of the day messing around right here, but we'll save that for another time. Now we cross."

Nine rocks, pre-arranged for dry passage, comprised a manageable route for fording the river called Mannequin Creek. Reily skipped over them in seconds. Boom teetered on each stone before reaching the other shore. The journey proved worth the trouble. A welcoming path followed the creek out of sight in each direction—a moss-topped, unbounded track through heaven. He stayed behind Reily as they ventured further, deeper, letting the bountiful grove embrace him like a long-lost brother.

9

Railroad Ravine. Collier's Rock. Towpath Cliff. The Lehigh River suited a rugged expedition—Reily's last great adventure before the first day of school.

The landmarks were behind them now as he, Wil, and Eddie lumbered along half-abandoned rail lines. Trees fenced the water on the other side of the tracks, yet every gap offered glimpses of churned, murky water from three days of intermittent thunderstorms. Trespassing came with risk, but minus a freight train or two, the solitude below Crum's Hill offered the reward of urban wilderness—close to the growing suburbs with the illusion of being a world away.

Reily listened to the rhythm of his boots crunching gravel. "How much farther do you want to go?"

"I'm up for stopping now. My head is killing me." Wil spoke from the rear of the caravan.

"Don't be a pussy," Eddie said.

Reily turned to face his crew. "Let's go as far as the dam. We can eat there and, if we want, hike on to the meadows."

Eddie adjusted his backpack straps. "It's not really a dam anymore. I'd call it a half-assed pile of cement and rebar."

"Like a B-52 bombed it." Wil chomped on an apple for dramatic effect.

Eddie shot him a disagreeable look. "If a B-52 plopped its payload, you wouldn't recognize the river. My old man said we should have dropped more bombs . . . and killed *all* the gooks."

Reily threw up his arms. "Do you have to say that?"

"What?" Eddie assumed a defensive pose. "You like Asians?"

Wil muffled a laugh. "I don't know many . . . but isn't your favorite show *Kung Fu*?"

Eddie fumed without an immediate comeback. Walking resumed. "My old man saw a lot of bad stuff in the war . . . buddies killed, babies killed. He didn't belong there. He had three months left in the reserves and kids at home when they sent him overseas in '66. Then he comes back, and his wife dies. I think that's why he's such a bastard most of the time."

A tinge of sadness struck Reily. It had to be hard to lose a mother and a spouse, plus, from all he heard, the Vietnam War had been a colossal waste of time and lives. "I can't believe it's over. We lost everything we supposedly fought for."

Wil sighed. "The futility of war." He gestured with a fishing rod clutched in his right hand. "The pictures in *Time* were pretty depressing . . . kids crying, people hanging on to helicopters, tanks rolling into Saigon. Everything undone just like that."

A green canoe diverted Reily's attention. A solo paddler jockeyed the boat upstream, working the water with agility. Art in fluid motion. The man waved. Reily waved back, and spotted what remained of the milldam. "We're almost there."

At the ruins, they jettisoned their packs and positioned themselves on the cement buttress that once anchored the dam. Wil dropped a line into the recirculating water below. Eddie munched on a mutilated bag of potato chips. Reily swigged from his canteen, laid back, and placed his hands under his head, appreciating marshmallow clouds presiding over a turning planet.

The paddler reappeared, playing in a line of riffles. He rode each chute until the current slowed, before powering into position to repeat the maneuver. Slowly he surfed their direction, before nosing into shore.

"How are you fellas doing?" The man, thirty years old or so, seemed genuine. His lean, compact build confirmed a pattern of frequent exercise.

"Fine, thanks," Reily said, serving as ambassador. "I never saw anyone canoe like that."

The man eased himself from the boat. "It's a lot of fun. Did you ever paddle?"

"Yes, well, in a lake—with two people in the boat."

"You're welcome to try it out." The man pointed at the canoe. "I can give you a few instructions. By the way, I'm Steve . . . Steve Patterson."

To be polite, Reily slid off the abutment and shook Steve's hand. "I'm Reily, and that's Wil and Eddie." Wil tipped his head. Eddie grunted.

After a quick lesson, Reily attempted to keep the one-person canoe straight and upright. No simple task, but after a while, he switched the paddle from side to side with confidence and challenged himself on a mild rapid. He ploughed through the muddy river, stirring his soul with the thrill of the maneuvers and the wet, earthy scents. His heart raced as he returned to the bank. "That was a blast."

Mr. Patterson looked pleased. "I thought you'd like it. Anyone else want to give it a shot?"

"No thanks." Wil failed to raise his head as he fussed with the line in his spool. Beside him, Eddie napped with a forearm shielding his eyes, and said nothing.

Mr. Patterson ignored the apathy. "I get out almost every weekend. If you want to paddle more, give me a call sometime. I don't mind sharing the river—in fact, I like introducing others to canoeing. It's a great sport." He fished through a container in his boat and handed Reily a business card. "That's my office number. I'm usually there."

Patterson pushed off and whisked away downstream, leaving Reily gawking in envy. Wil returned to the terrestrial present, hooking his line on an eyelet of the fishing rod. Eddie stirred.

Reily peeled and devoured a hard-boiled egg he had stowed. "How about we push on? The meadows aren't much further."

"Good by me." Wil began to self-organize.

Eddie grunted again—atypical sullenness for the big guy.

Underway, Reily engaged him. "My dad told me that the Kemp Farm has been sold. He saw a surveyor there."

"That spews," Eddie said. "They better not mess with the pond."

"Dad thinks they'll build houses, but who knows how many. Some of the ground is too soggy."

"It won't be the same." Eddie made a monster face. "I want to tear 'em up."

Wil heard the comment. "Easy, avenger man. Progress—so to speak—is inevitable."

Eddie faked a blitzing tackle. "Who made you God?"

Wil strolled onward, undeterred. "I'm self-appointed."

Reily regarded both of them, each smug and self-assured but with unique qualities. Regardless of their idiosyncrasies, they were epic friends, sun-sweltered and larger than life on this August afternoon.

"I forgot to tell you guys about the wooden stakes I saw on my hike with Colleen. They were spread out in the woods and definitely marking something. One of them said Eastern Power LLC."

Wil halted. "Wait a minute. I read another story in the newspaper about that lake coming to Northampton County . . . I'm pretty sure that was the name of the company."

Eddie laughed. "You read the paper? What a blockhead."

Wil kicked dirt at Eddie. "Shut up, doofus. Maybe someday you'll *learn* to read."

Reily imagined Hoover Dam looming over his town. "I have a bad feeling about whatever they're up to in our woods."

An expansive field, dubbed "the meadows" by locals, spread out east of the tracks. Coppery sedges and pioneer sumacs with reddening clusters of fuzzy fruit fashioned an austere scene his mother might have painted. Reily traipsed across flat land where a foundry once forged nails and heavy wire. Burnt logs indicated a popular place to stage camp, atop ground deadened by its industrial past.

Reily cleared stones with his boot. "Let's pitch the tent here."

Eddie dropped the pack from his back. "You're making dinner since I carried the heaviest load."

"Only if Wil puts the tent up."

Wil folded his arms in defiance. "I'm in charge of the fire."

"Whatever," Reily said. "You two don't behave, I'm going to withhold your rations."

Eddie glared. "Fat chance, Watters."

His friends sat around a small campfire, entranced by the aroma of bubbling beef stew and the peaceful evening glow of an exceptional day nearly gone. How many moments like this did they have left? Soon there could be jobs, maybe girlfriends, to suck away freedom. When Reily shared such cogitations at home, his dad would snicker and say not to worry so much. *If only it were that easy.*

Eddie grabbed a bowl and spoon from the pile of provisions. "I can't wait any longer. I'm going in."

"Don't take it all." Wil uttered the warning from a beach towel— afraid to sully the backside of shorts too white.

The site became soundless, the meal requiring their utmost attention.

"Tasty." Eddie showed an empty bowl and delinquent face. "Better wash it down with a splash."

Reily evaluated his fellow adventurer. "You didn't."

Wil shook his head. "He did."

Eddie revealed a medicine bottle, void of cough syrup and filled with hard liquor. "This will make you feel better than a hot night with Colleen Mills." He laughed maniacally at the dumb comparison, before reaching into his mammoth pack for surely more contraband. Instead, he brought forth a sketchpad and pencil. "I think I'll do a bit of drawing to accompany my hooch."

Stars illumined the sky one by one through the astral drift of city lights. Wil read by the beam of a flashlight. Eddie lined an opportune masterwork. Reily regarded them in their self-contentment, before volunteering to wash dishes. He ambled to the river, waiting for a locomotive lacking boxcars to grumble past. At the water's edge, a faint breeze refreshed him while his hands scrubbed and rinsed to thoughts about crazy friends, a certain girl, and the surprises, exciting or mundane, tomorrow might bring.

Every miraculous day chanced a new experience or situation. Memories to be born and someday relived.

10

For a city full of hot air and red tape, Washington, D.C. boasted the breezy deportment of a European city. The pageantry of buildings gratified Merle, but the trash-filled tidal basin left him malcontent.

With the adjournment of the annual meeting of the professional society, he self-piloted on a solo tour of the nation's capital. Statues and monuments, impregnated with historical significance, tickled his craving for yesteryear. At Lincoln's feet, he all but wept—overcome by the weight of antiquity.

By the halls of the Smithsonian, Merle's feet fatigued from shipping his middle-aged corpse over miles of hardscape. Saddled bunions softened at a portrait of Teddy Roosevelt on horseback. Herbert Hoover, albeit more corpulent, resembled his father or the photos thereof. Notwithstanding the Democratic affiliation, Franklin Roosevelt had admirable gumption. His painted countenance spoke to Merle, one modernizer to another.

Panels about the Great Depression exhumed the imposed frugality he had experienced as a youngster, including rationing during the war. The Works Progress Administration and the Public Works Administration put millions of people back to work, but their greatest achievement proved to be infrastructure—from airfields and bridges to the mightiest of dams. Such majestic edifices were a dying breed. American ingenuity had languished.

Merle liked Howard Miller's Westinghouse wartime poster. The female worker flexed her muscle with the caption "We Can Do It!" It allied with his faith in the promise, the latent potential, of the not so fainthearted. In another room rife with memorabilia, a lifejacket from the Titanic told a cautionary tale about the perils of arrogance. The John Deere plow and the Conestoga wagon better communicated his commercial ethos. Some might call them slow and plodding, but, in his eyes, they were nobly persistent and resilient—hunkered down for the long haul.

A sign inside the portico of the National Museum of Natural History expressed its mission: "Understanding the *natural* world and our place *in* it." Merle sneezed, spraying an aerosol of germs, allergic to the inscribed words. Man's place, his overarching part in the balance of things, bore little ambiguity. *We build the future.*

Deep down, Merle knew that to be a half-truth. Man could also distort, disrupt, and destroy. You had to have the gift of vision. He, afflicted with both myopia and hyperopia, questioned the limits of human discernment.

11

Reily's first week of high school passed in a flash, proving less taxing than he had presumed. He shared a class with Colleen and sat with her at lunch every day. The relationship hummed.

The next Monday, she shocked him at the end of first period.

"Do you want to come over after school? I have to show you my bedroom. I just painted it."

Reily reddened. "Sure, that'd be really cool." He was afraid he sounded like a dork.

In third period, he sat next to Boom and found a chance to tell him about his impending visit to Colleen's house. "I've only been there once—and I didn't go inside."

Boom nodded with too much enthusiasm. "Soon, you two will be engaged."

"Not so fast. We've only been seeing each other for a few weeks."

The teacher raised his eyebrows and scowled. "Is there something you'd like to announce to the rest of us, Mr. Watters?"

Reily slouched lower in his seat. "No, Mr. Kreider. Nothing to report." His classmates chuckled. The biology teacher could be stern, but, he mostly raved with enthusiasm about all things science. Some of the kids made fun of Kreider and his scruffy beard. Reily found him interesting, likeable.

A lesson started about the Linnaean taxonomic system. As the instructor chalked "genus" on the blackboard, a towering, vivacious senior slipped in the door: Cindy Sutherland, swim team star.

"Cynthia's going to join us periodically this year," Mr. Kreider said. "She plans to major in environmental science in college and will serve as my assistant and tutor for labs and other activities."

Reily glanced at Boom. Boom seemed hypnotized, his hands locked to the top of the desk. Cindy stood straight as a board, poised and mature. She smiled in their direction.

In the hall after class, Boom went wild. "Reily, can you believe it? We will see Cindy every day. And she smiled at us, did you see that?"

"Be quiet. She might hear you. You have to keep your cool." Reily pulled him toward his locker. "Don't forget, she's an upperclassman. She might not be interested in your attention."

"No Reily, you must be positive. You never know." Boom's eyes broadcasted an inextinguishable fervor.

"Okay, but don't say I didn't warn you." A sudden push from behind jostled Reily. He swiveled to find big Eddie laughing at him. "Very funny, Knisely. What's going on?"

"I'm off to World Cultures. I think we're talking about Africa or something dumb."

Boom walked away, stone-faced.

Reily shot Eddie a sideways glance. "That wasn't nice."

"What? Seriously, that's what we're covering."

"I have to get to English." Reily left Eddie, letting him sulk alone. He had known Eddie since fourth grade, but the prejudices of the overgrown boob remained hidden until recent months.

The crowded hallway and the din of slamming lockers unsettled him. *Why did the school always smell like an alcohol swab?* He pined for the creek—the serene and simple existence beside the water. The good life.

Reily smoldered. The pleasant heat within him intensified the closer he came to Colleen's house. By the time he arrived, perspiration pooled in his armpits. Self-consciousness made him perspire more. *Get a grip, dude.*

He positioned his bike on the carport, took a hard breath, and knocked on the side door. He heard footsteps inside, followed by a lovely presence behind the screen.

"You made it." Reily perceived a dash of joviality in her voice. With Colleen, glee did not come easy.

"Sorry. I had to finish my geometry homework." *Boy, did that sound goofy.*

She opened the flimsy door for him. "Likely story, but I'll let you in anyway."

A messy kitchen connected to a living room with a musty odor. Sparse windows and bulky drapes created dim and drab confines, but Colleen on the sofa brightened things up.

"This is my house," she announced. "Pretty boring, huh?"

"Not at all. Where is everybody?"

"You mean my mom?"

"Yeah, sorry." *You're such an idiot, Watters.*

"She's on late shift this week. She won't be home until after ten."

"Oh." He remained standing while Colleen lounged and twirled her hair.

"You're allowed to sit down." She patted the upholstery beside her.

"Okay." Reily lowered himself on an unsupportive cushion, struggling to retain a suave posture.

"Do you want something to drink? You look warm."

"No, I'm fine. Thanks."

"I want a Coke. Be right back." She hurried from the room. He noticed the delightful contours of her form-fitting terry cloth shorts.

When Colleen returned, she stood in front of him, eager, impatient. "What should we do?" A glass soda bottle hung from her right hand. He sensed that when it came to guys, she directed the course of events under a pretense of democracy.

He considered television, but making out to game shows lacked romantic quality. "Did you say you painted your room?" *Oh no, that came off too forward.*

"Yep, but I'll warn you, it's different." She offered her other hand. "Follow me."

His hand tingled as she tugged him toward the intimate lair.

A black dresser abutted a wall with a wide mirror. Shag carpet in a light shade of blue covered the floor and muted all sound. A modern floor lamp reached from a corner, beside a single bed with stuffed animals and a zebra-striped comforter.

"The room used to be boring white." Colleen scanned him for a reaction.

Reily squeezed her hand, still in his grasp. "It's funky . . . and I mean that in a good way." He further evaluated the surroundings. A flowery hint of perfume hung in the small quarters. "What do they call this shade of yellow?"

"Electric banana."

They both laughed.

Colleen set her Coke on a nightstand and scooched onto the bed. Reily took the cue. Felonious guilt overcame him. *Rites of passage shouldn't feel so wrong.* His girl positioned herself to invite advance and he moved close, his prostrate body parallel to hers. Lips touched and hands caressed, moral worries cast aside.

Hours elapsed. Hunger bore no match to ravenous, amorous pleasure. His heart fluttered, his mind floated. Colleen became the center of a temporary cosmos.

Physicality interspersed with breathy quips of quirky conversation. Red hearts on underwear. Locking mechanisms of bras. A potential hickey on Reily's neck. Banter birthed more profound insights. Colleen loved their hike, but hated her dad. Now, her mom, aka Vicki, had a boyfriend—a real creep—who rode a Harley and thought he lived in the 1950s.

Darkening shadows triggered panic. Reily leapt from the mattress and retrieved his garments littered upon the floor. Once composed, he gave Colleen frothy, lasting lip-to-lip inspiration. "See you at school."

The sun had set and he had only minutes to navigate home before nightfall. He felt invincible jockeying his bike through the cool twilight.

The final days of astronomical summer were proving to be truly stellar.

12

Boom galloped through the forested sanctuary near Reily's home. Branches rushed by. Sunshine flickered. Leaves eased into new colors, feeding on every exhalation. He imagined the trees as spectators, cheering him to a record finish. His labored breath told him otherwise. *More training required.*

When the land rose, he braked and rested—new running shoes streaked with moss and mud. Sweat became glue for biological fragments, but the grime only primed him. Boom wanted more miles to conquer.

Now he walked, in giant strides, to probe further into the tenacious terrain. The constant *whish* of the creek became less noticeable as he climbed, until it ceased. The topography formed a canyon and, at the bottom, the watercourse morphed into a swimmable pond. A heavy rope hung from a tree and almost touched the still water. The setting reminded him of the beautiful paintings in Reily's house.

Boom guessed there might be more surprises as he hiked further. The trail had ended at the swimming hole, but still he followed the creek, sorry to trample whatever lay unseen. Let other kids sleep away the morning. *He* preferred unaccompanied quests.

On the slopes of the creek, evergreens multiplied. Away from the water, on the undulating highlands, deciduous trees reigned. The forest became a mosaic of layers and textures bestowing immeasurable tidings.

The stream narrowed, the gradient increased. The shallow currents had more to say. Reily told him that the waters spoke, but few people took the time to interpret their language. Boom tried, straining to differentiate the joyful babble. *Who couldn't be happy in such a place?*

The sound escalated. A waterfall appeared, like a photograph from the pages of a fancy calendar. Upward he scrambled. Above the picturesque plunge, he inhaled the chilled, electrified air.

The land began to level off as the gentle banks of the creek grew rocky. Boom investigated. Here, he could nearly leap across the water. He prepared to lunge, but recoiled—a thick, black snake probed the crevices ten feet away. Cobra fears arose, but they did not live in North America. The snake flicked its tongue, inspecting the surroundings. It slithered and stopped, and slithered some more, moving along at a reptile's pace to savor the autumn day.

Boom noted the snake's glossy sheen and coloration, and approximated its size. Watching, he felt a kindred connection. No one liked snakes. They had it tough, like a black kid in Whiteville. Maybe it, too, found autonomy in remote, vitalizing places.

13

Coach Finn left the natatorium to counsel a floundering member of the swim team. Reily empathized with the disinterested senior. Mediocrity grew tiresome.

In the free-for-all waning minutes of the optional, pre-season morning practice, Reily treaded water where the bottom of the pool sloped into the twelve-foot end of their training rectangle. The high dive loomed pastel bright, yet still frightening.

Reily's fear of tall places could be traced to a tree climbing incident with his loving sister. She denied intentionally stomping on his five-year-old fingers, but, to this day, he believed otherwise. In agony, he had inadvertently released his grip and pinballed through the branches until he slammed face-first against the ground, limbs beaten and bloodied.

Cindy Sutherland must have escaped similar childhood trauma. Before him, she ascended the ladder to a horrific height, hesitated, and projected herself toward the ceiling in a seamless catapult. A second later, she speared the water's surface with barely a splash—teenager turned blue-breasted booby. She made diving look easy.

Reily tuned out the horseplay of teammates and concentrated on mustering enough courage to follow Cindy's fearless act, only he intended to do it feet first. He exited the pool, and approached the tower of terror, sizing its menacing dimensions. Hand over hand he rose, trying to let the demons slip away.

At the pinnacle of vertical success, the Matterhorn and Mount Everest came to mind. Kilimanjaro with emphasis on *Kil.* The ridiculous elevation prompted an onset of vertigo and sheer fright, but he couldn't back down due to a danger-driven physical inability to reverse direction. The sooner the torture ended, the better.

Reily managed one step . . . and another. The board flexed above a familiar, but far away, translucent crash pad. The end of the plank waited. He advanced. The horizon dipped. He wobbled and tripped. Freefall. Flailing toward impact.

An awkward entry. A reverberating whack. Searing pain. He struggled to the side of the pool where Cindy and another swimmate helped him from the water, laying him on the cold, hard edge. Out of focus, they checked his body for injuries.

"I never heard a sound like that," Cindy's visage spoke, leaning over him.

Her male companion laughed. "Man, it was like a beaver's tail slapping a pond. That had to hurt."

Indeed, it had. Reily's side and shoulder throbbed with a distinct exterior numbness. His clammy skin ached with every reconstruction of the bad dream sequence. He stood gingerly and thanked the young emergency responders. His attempt at bravery and self-improvement had failed miserably, but he had survived.

14

Wil watched the clock inside the library. A stooped, stern, mannish woman stamped a pregnant lady's outgoing stack of books. Two kids giggled in a far aisle. The scuffed cover of his civics textbook taunted him about a reading assignment unread, but he could only think of Kelly Bingham.

Their romance erupted ten days ago, leaving minimal time to share the sordid details with Reily. Ninth grade supplied surprising abundance in its opening weeks, but nothing compared to the astounding advances of a single-minded cheerleader two grades above. Even with such spicy distractions, he missed the camaraderie of his best friend.

Why Kelly had chosen him was mystifying. Everyone knew she dated the high school fullback, but under the lights at Weyant Park, she had lingered. Chitchat led to a hands-on shooting lesson. Then other lessons. His pulse quickened merely thinking about it.

While he waited, he pretended to read. A paragraph about the free press stirred daydreams of journalism. Wil pictured the newsroom in *The Mary Tyler Moore Show*, but had trouble seeing himself in any of the characters.

By 2:15, he became restless and began to doubt Kelly's promise to meet. He strolled and scanned the aisles for any book worth examining. Several titles on fishing stole his interest, and a book on dams and rivers. Iconic photos of the Grand Coulee and Glen Canyon stood out. One, of the Ludington Pumped Storage Project, showed a reservoir above the shores of Lake Michigan. The image and terminology resurrected the story of a possible hydroelectric dam in Northampton County. Reily had found stakes near their coveted creek. The matter deserved more investigation.

In minutes, Wil rooted through newspapers that the stern woman, friendly after all, helped him find. There were actually two stories about the hydroelectric deal. He jotted notes with a pencil onto index cards given to him by his new elderly friend. He had the dam book with him, too, and skimmed it for useful information.

The micro-research project subsumed him. He had lost hope of Kelly's showing. At 3:10, he jammed the book into its rightful place on the shelf and turned to leave. At the end of the row, he all but collided with a short, dirty blonde girl with mid-length hair and a devious smile. She nudged him to the corner.

"Sorry I'm late." Kelly pressed against him, fluttering her lashes for forgiveness.

The method worked. "That's okay. I didn't mind hanging out here."

"Troy took me to the mall. I couldn't escape."

Wil sensed inherent weakness within. A tiny silver heart glittered on each of her earlobes. *Such sumptuous auricles.* "I'm glad you showed up."

Kelly rose up and kissed him in a wet, provocative style. "There . . . was it worth the wait?"

"Yep." He could barely get the word out of his mouth.

She took his hand and dragged him to the under-trafficked literature section. "Kiss me more." Her words sounded like a demand.

Wil obliged. After several minutes, his jaw became sore though he tingled throughout. A second librarian pushed a cart their direction, paused and glared, terminating their clandestine session. "We better go."

Kelly adjusted her hair. "I can't. I have a paper due next week about a current event and I have no clue what I'm going to write about."

Her forlorn plight sparked an idea. Wil reached for his notecards. "I have a suggestion."

Kelly thanked him for the unique topic by delivering one more smacker. As Wil opened his eyes, a junior he recognized stared at the two of them. "Hey, isn't he on the football team?"

Kelly flushed. "You better get out of here."

Wil backpedaled. "Call me."

"I'll try."

He gleaned doubt in her assertion, and inklings of trouble yet to come.

Say of the Day: liability.

15

Reily's baited hook bounced through a small channel established by two defiant rocks challenging the supremacy of water. From afar, raveled twists and rumples gave the impression of a translucent veil, separating and splicing as it slipped onward, restless yet reunified. A violent tussle interrupted existential musings.

"Damn, that's a fighter. Bring her in."

Reily needed no instruction from Wil. The line danced and he kept the rod tip low, retrieving his quarry in quick cranks of the reel. He led the fish to the mud and roots on the Mannequin's edge, and pulled it from the water.

"What the heck is it?" Camouflaged bars covered a tapered, toadish body. The pulsating thing eyed-in at seven inches.

"That would be a mottled sculpin." Wil scrutinized the catch. "I never caught one except in a minnow seine. Nice going, Watters."

On this lower reach, vertical banks made mucky spots where the soil crumbled away. Reily sank to his ankles, reaching for the needle-nosed pliers in his kit ashore. He wiggled the hook free from the prehistoric creature. Wil's ID had to be accurate—when it came to angling and aquatic matters, Wil knew more than *Encyclopedia Britannica*.

Reily watched, mesmerized, as the released fish scuttled through the shallows, dorsal parts exposed before vanishing in the depths.

Wil gawked too. "It swims worse than you."

"Very funny. Hey, did I tell you Boom quit the swim team?"

"Nope." Wil dug for a worm from a white cardboard carton. "Why did he do that?"

"Said he wants to focus on running." Reily tightened the drag on his reel. "Our first regular practice is next week. He won't be able to put his man moves on Cindy Sutherland."

"She's big league."

"I know, but she acts interested. Must be his accent."

"He'll be a legend if he lands her, almost on par with my liberties with Kelly Bingham."

"You wish."

Wil exhaled in an arrogant way. "Never doubt the love meister. We've enjoyed two lusty encounters." He shared details of his hazardous achievement—a perilous tale told in two parts.

Reily questioned the story. For Wil's sake, he sure wished it were a fantasy. "You do know who she dates . . ."

"Dude, don't worry." Wil played out more line. "Did you see that rise? They get extra hungry this time of year.

Reily rubbed his side, still bruised and tender from the high dive catastrophe. "If Troy Troxell lets you live, I sense a good luck streak. You and Kelly, Boom and Cindy, me and Colleen . . ." He flipped the bail on his spinning reel and cast with a flick of his wrist, floating the line across a low-hanging branch. "Dang. I'm snagged."

Wil swallowed a laugh. "Some luck. You might have jinxed us." He took a turn finding his target, employing a sidearm toss. The bait landed in the middle of a hole, a scene of stirrings moments before.

"Good cast." His friend skipped the enticement over the stream bottom and let it return with the current, further and deeper. "I forgot to tell you. I penned a poem for Colleen."

Wil brought in the line, surrendering the round—a short-lived stalemate between man and fish. "What a stud. Writing prose for your lady. I have to get you out more, toughen you up. Pretty soon, you'll be buying opera tickets or taking dance lessons."

Reily pushed the hair from his eyes and assessed Wil. "Wait a minute. Who's the writer wannabe?"

"You mean taking on powerful politicians and corporations? Doesn't get much tougher than that."

"Valid point. Nothing wimpy about serious writing." Wil had the right attitude for it, too. Reily waded toward the entanglement of his making, winding in the slack proving impossible to unravel. He severed the line in defeat—a customary sacrament of many outings.

Wil broke down his rod, and put the bait and accessories into a knapsack. They both knew that a wary angler should never push his luck. "When are you going to show me Eddie's hoard?"

Reily envisioned food and alcohol. "Oh, the magazines. Hmm. I should be able to find them. We have to head upstream." In his mind, he saw the sprawling tree flexing its might and secrets in the wide, flat tapestry of woods.

"I forgot to tell you, I got more of the scoop." Wil's voice deepened as they walked. "They plan to dam up this very creek near the headwaters. You were right about the name of the company, Eastern Power. There are three partners, three dudes, planning the thing. It will be pumped storage."

Reily listened while he took in the familiar, nevertheless splendid, surroundings on the lukewarm, late afternoon. "What does that mean?"

"They'll make a big dam fifty-feet tall, and an umpteen-acre impoundment. The creek water will flow into it, but they'll also pump water from the Lehigh River though a pipeline to fill it up."

"I don't get it . . . they want to make a lake?"

"The dam will have turbines and they'll release the water during the day to make hydroelectricity. They'll use more electricity to pump the water into the lake, but they can sell the electricity for more money during the day."

"Good investigating. Where'd you learn all this?"

"The library. I had time to kill waiting for Kelly." Wil sighed and pretended to clutch his heart.

Reily feared a daily surge might obliterate the creek. A reservoir could flood a huge area.

"Are we getting close?"

"I think so." The understory thinned as the overstory sprawled. A faint breeze agitated the leaves, whispering confirmation. "That's it, I'm pretty sure. Over there." Reily hustled for the gargantuan tree and the luring indentation at its base.

Wil marched forth greedily.

Reily pointed. "Reach in that gap."

Wil stooped and probed with an arm. "Nothing. Eddie must have moved the riches."

Reily had no chance for disappointment, for a bewildering image bounded his way—a large, fluffy, dirty canine.

Wil inched backwards. "What the hell—"

The beast arrived, its tail declaring unconditional surrender.

Reily knelt on the cool ground and let the dog sniff his outreached hand. The animal reciprocated by licking his arm and face, leaving a film of gooey saliva. Although well-soiled, the dog retained vigor and exuberance, as if destiny designed it for this single meeting.

Wil relaxed. "It doesn't have a collar."

"Nope." Reily kneaded the pup's soft head, admiring its white and tawny coat. "I wonder if it's lost."

"You mean *he*. I think it's a boy."

Reily zipped his dad's old flight jacket. The dog cocked its head at the sound. "We have to go, but I hate to leave him."

"If you love something, let it go. If it returns, it's yours. If it doesn't, it wasn't."

"Well said, for a junior high student. But we *should* give him a temporary name."

They started walking east to intersect the road back to the neighborhood. The dog followed—a tail to the two amigos.

Reily stewed through options. "How about Cousteau . . . as in Jacques Cousteau?"

"The dog will be scarred for life. He lives on land, *not* in the sea."

Animals had special meaning to Reily, akin to Saint Francis seeing all creatures as his siblings, although sometimes Reily liked animals better than his own sister. "Alright, how's this? Marlin as in Marlin Perkins, the TV wildlife guy."

"Stupid, but acceptable." Wil hiked up his sweatpants, stretched from daily wear.

The dog paralleled Reily. "Hey Marlin, do you like *Wild Kingdom*?" The dog moved closer, happiness in motion. "I guess that's a yes."

Meanwhile, Wil, in standard sloppy-go-lucky mode, chewed a birch twig and hummed a tune by The Band . . . a cool ditty about a girl named Fanny.

Pushed by the setting sun, Reily lengthened his strides, his gangly wrists protruding from the arms of the jacket. He wondered what his parents would say about adopting a strange dog. Their last dog, a spaniel, died of old age five years earlier. They hadn't considered another addition to the family.

Wet shoes tapped a tempo on crumbling pavement. Marlin oozed excitement, his disposition contagious. They made quite a trio . . . a pair of old friends, plus one, hairy and new, fortified by fresh air and the beneficial rigors of independent living.

16

The shortening days sucked, in Eddie's opinion. Fall came out of nowhere, but the smorgasbord of seasonal colors made it acceptable. Before him, the Watters house glowed like the White House. It felt like a second home.

Reily's mom welcomed him, as did the new dog. It looked like Lassie with a shorter nose. Eddie tasted the scent of steaks. *They always have the best food.*

"I brought my sketchbook and watercolor kit, like you said."

Karen Watters beamed. "Good. Go say hi to Reily. I'll finish cleaning up, and then we can get started."

Eddie stumbled into Reily's room. The lovesick idiot held up a phone dangling a spiral cord, and mouthed that Colleen occupied the other end of the line. Eddie sat on the corner of the bed in disgust, the burdened mattress causing an audible squeak. "You two may as well be married."

While Reily cooed with his dove, Eddie examined the bookshelf above an antique desk. The Hardy Boys he had heard of, but not *Leaves of Grass*. A Lowenbrau beer stein came from one of Mr. Watters's trips to Germany. A stack of 8-track tapes included many bands Eddie liked, except for the Jackson Five.

Reily hung up. "Sorry about that."

"About time. You two are inseparable."

Reily stood and adjusted the items Eddie had displaced. "I haven't seen her for three days—except at school."

"My heart breaks . . ."

Marlin barged into the bedroom and leapt onto the bed, demanding Reily's attention. His tail dusted Eddie's face.

Eddie wiped hairs from his mouth. "That's disgusting."

Reily rubbed Marlin's ears. "He knows you need exfoliated . . . scrubbed of bad thoughts and deeds."

Eddie prepared to pummel his friend.

Reily raised his arms to deflect imminent blows. "I'm only kidding. Marlin likes you. I can tell."

Eddie unclenched his fist. "He's a cool dog. Nobody claimed him?"

"We checked at the Humane Society. Nothing."

"Weird." Eddie twisted his neck each direction, releasing a chorus of crackling vertebrae. "You found him at the creek?"

"Immaculate arrival. He came out of nowhere. We were by the tree. The tree where you hid . . ." Reily lowered his voice, "the magazines."

Eddie nodded. "They weren't there, were they?"

Reily sulked. "You could have told me."

"I moved them—for convenience. And safekeeping."

Mrs. Watters summoned him from the hallway.

Eddie sprang to attention. "Got to go, Jethro, but don't worry, I'll let you peek at them again."

Reily elbowed him toward the door. "Go paint the world, Picasso."

The Watters's summer kitchen doubled as an art studio. Reily's mom had two freestanding easels, side-by-side, ready for teaching. She gave Eddie artistic advice numerous times, but never regular lessons. He hoped she saw him as a worthy student.

Overhead lighting set the room ablaze while Mrs. Watters reviewed the essentials—paints, paint trays, brushes, spray bottles, and mason jars half-filled with water. "I usually stretch the watercolor paper, but, for now, we'll use tacked sheets." She had a springy demeanor in her instruction. Eddie thought of her as a kind of substitute mom. His own mother had died of breast cancer a day before his seventh birthday.

He marveled at the variety of pigments. "Mrs. Watters, which shade of brown should I use?"

"Please Eddie, you can call me Karen." Mrs. W. made him feel like an equal. An uplifting gleam and medium-length, sandy brown hair complemented her slender stature. At the top of each easel, she taped matching photos of the Kemp Farm bathed in winter light. "Go with burnt sienna and raw umber. We'll use them for the fields and buildings—but not yet."

An hour later, a painting took form. A cobalt sky backed proportioned, penciled outlines of a house, barn, and corncrib. A sliver of the pond occupied the foreground. On the left side of the scene, Eddie put final touches on the driveway and road, using light applications of Payne's grey.

Karen stood behind him, evaluating the work. "Masterful . . . but watch the intensity of the blue. It's fine, but in the future, you might lighten it slightly."

Eddie made a mental note and relished his progress. The creative process absorbed him.

He felt different . . . renewed and refurbished from this singular kickass session.

17

Merle gaped across the quadrilateral chasm that once sourced slate to roofs up and down the Atlantic seaboard. His mind flashed to the Maine coast, and a walk long ago with a temporary fiancée along maritime cliffs buffeted by moody swells. The present, calmer void presented a grievous danger, but he foresaw fancy homes positioned to view the surreal, cerulean water.

"The authority lands encircle the quarry, Mr. Darkes." The tubby authority representative wore coveralls with his name monogrammed on the breast pocket. The man gestured casually at the edge, as if he might take a leap. "Our property cups this whole valley."

"My surveyors verified that, but I wanted to see things firsthand." The wheels whirled in Merle's ovate head. While an existing hazard, the pit meant greater water storage—more capacity, more profit. "When does the board vote?"

Intermittent leaves alighted and tumbled to a soggy fate, distracting the local official. "Sure is a long drop."

"What about the board?" Merle asked, louder.

"Sorry . . . not until the nineteenth of November. That's the quarterly meeting."

"And you think there's concurrence around the proposed terms of the contract?"

Beating wings drew the man's attention overhead. "Those are wood ducks."

"Please, can we discuss the matter at hand?" *Locals moved at sloth speed.* "I have an appointment with my consulting attorney this afternoon and would like to give him an update."

"Oh, I think everyone feels good about what you've spelled out. They're already talking about water system upgrades and purchasing new dump trucks for winter maintenance."

Merle found the enthusiasm reassuring.

The return trek to their respective vehicles tested his cardiovascular fitness. With the home pool drained and closed until May, his exercise repertoire had dissolved.

"What the—" Ten yards ahead, his de facto guide lurched backwards.

Merle approached, panicked. "What's the matter?" The human Butterball heaved, stooped over, with hands on his knees. Merle scavenged his brain for instructions should CPR be required.

"Over there . . . helluva black snake. I almost squashed it."

Nothing moved. Merle scanned the ground until he spied the serpent, stretched out only feet away. "Jesus, that's huge." He despised snakes. As a child, a neighbor let him hold a garter snake, only to have it squirt a foul musk on his Sunday dress shirt. "Is it poisonous?"

The authority man's posture normalized. "Nope, they don't hurt nothing, except rodents and such."

The assertion brought scant comfort. Besides a few deer and box turtles ready for retirement, wildlife seemed MIA in the hydro project fairway. "I'm glad they're not prevalent," Merle said.

His companion on the impromptu safari bore a crafty smile. "Oh, you see 'em here and there. Part of the natural order."

If Merle had dominion over the earth, he would order them *gone*— permanently exiled and vanquished.

18

Mr. Kreider used a pointer to reference an oversized illustration. "The cell membrane is what protects the cell from everything around it." The teacher wielded the implement like a mad scientist, but without the white frock. His sand-hued, button-down shirt gave him the air of a college professor leading research in the field. He tapped on the blackboard as he spoke. "Most cells also contain a mitochondrion, essentially the power plant for cellular activities."

Boom labeled the parts on his worksheet. He raised his head and caught Cindy Sutherland looking at him. He had to grin. With her ravishing cells and tight, white sweater, his mitochondria were poised to light up a city.

"But cells called prokaryotes don't need mitochondria. They get their energy elsewhere." Mr. Kreider scanned the room to gauge attention. "More on them in the coming weeks."

Boom extended his study of Cindy . . . sculpted cheekbones, supple ears, parabolic nose. He never had a girlfriend, but he wanted to make her his. Her inquisitiveness and intelligence paired well with her beauty. Past Cindy's Nordic braids, wildlife posters plastered the classroom wall. One depicted eastern songbirds, while another presented the frogs of Pennsylvania. A third poster, above Reily's head, exhibited the non-venomous snakes collection.

After the bell abbreviated the lesson, Boom wove through the rows of chairs to investigate the latter poster. Cindy approached from the side, and his respiration accelerated. "Do you know these kinds?" He brushed his finger across two species with black coloration—the eastern rat snake and northern black racer.

Cindy leaned in to read the descriptions. "No, but they're big. It says they can both be over six feet." Eagerness showed. She smelled sweeter than the jasmine that grew behind his house on the other continent.

"I believe I saw one of these snakes on a hike."

Cindy remained close. "Do you like to hike?" She peered into his eyes, as if pleading for a positive response.

"I do, very much. Reily showed me a good place."

"Let's go there sometime."

Boom swallowed. "Okay, certainly."

"I better get to class." Cindy backed away. "I miss seeing you at swim practice."

"Yes, wonderful." *That didn't make any sense.* With dueling thoughts, he considered the poster again.

Mr. Kreider organized his desk at the front of the room. "Ben, you're going to be late for next period."

"Thanks Mr. Kreider, but I have early lunch." Boom returned his attention to the illustrations on the wall. "Do you know things about snakes?"

The teacher strolled his direction, brow furrowed, as if the question deserved a scholarly response. "What do you want to know?"

"These two black snakes . . . are they found around here?"

Mr. Kreider scratched his beard before answering. "The black racer is uncommon, from my experience. I have seen them in other areas, but not nearby. You typically can find rat snakes around old buildings and farms. Forests, too." He crossed his arms. "Why do you ask?"

"I encountered one of them. Along Mannequin Creek."

"Are you sure it wasn't the northern water snake?" Kreider gestured with a shoulder to where the species occupied the poster.

Boom shook his head. "No, this snake was very dark."

"I don't advise harassing wild animals, but if you see it again, there's an easy way to differentiate the two black snakes. The racer has a gray belly. The rat, a light one."

Students began to trickle into class. Boom absorbed the identification tip.

Mr. Kreider patted Boom on the back, and chuckled. "Good luck. I hope it rolls over for you."

Colleen suppressed a smile as she watched Reily suck the last lumps of a milkshake with amplified gurgling from across the lunch table. Other students cast annoyed glances, but such awkward acts didn't faze her. The devotion of a person like Reily had never happened to her before. His positive, humble personality improved her moods, and so did his kisses, although he could be overattentive on occasion.

Her shaggy boyfriend turned serious. "What else did Kelly say?"

"I could barely hear her, but she whispered something about Troy planning to do something to Wil. She said he knows that Wil hit on her."

"From what Wil tells me, she's twisting reality. She came on to him big time." Reily wiped chocolate residue from his mouth with a paper napkin. "I'm not saying he hasn't enjoyed it." He flaunted his dark brown eyes.

"He better be careful. Troy's a tank." She paused to fix her hair tie. "He'll have the whole football team after him."

"Yeah, I'm worried about him." Reily rubbed his forehead, and then leaned back, as if switching a gear. "Can we see each other this weekend?"

"Do you want to bowl?"

"I stink at bowling, but sure."

So agreeable. She reached for his hand. "I also want you to take me exploring again. Like we did in the summer."

Reily brightened. "Anytime. Maybe Saturday afternoon. We could bowl Friday night. I promised Dad I'd help with yard work on Sunday."

Colleen liked how he organized things, and how he did so automatically. Chaos governed her life. "Tell me where and when, and I'll escape."

Her unintentionally suave sophomore gathered his trash, and hers, his flannel shirt frayed and worn, the sleeves too short. "I look forward to our adventure, Ms. Mills. Talk to you later?"

"Of course." She watched him amble away, lost in the cafeteria, as if he were on his own virtuous planet. Reily's world.

19

The morning meet versus Quakertown left Reily wondering how Quakers were peace-loving people. A locker room skirmish required intervention by opposing coaches. Mr. Finn almost blew a swim bladder.

From the bus window, rounded hay bales lay scattered across fields as if waiting for something to do. A bowling alley on the right side of Route 309 looked abandoned this Saturday morning, but in better shape than the decrepit lanes where Colleen validated her rolling talents the night before. A billboard promoted the local Kawasaki motorcycle shop. He thought of Eddie's Yamaha, ridden on the rare occasion it would start. The big lug raced down neighborhood streets, and through the sacred woods. He lectured Eddie multiple times to keep away from the Mannequin, but Reily understood—100 cc's delivered one heckuva ride.

Back at school, teammates shuffled away, numb from losing or early rising. Reily retrieved his bike and pedaled for home, the loyal duffel draped over his back, thighs already tight and tired.

Dad welcomed him at the house, still in his bathrobe and anchored at the kitchen table paying bills. "How was the first meet?"

"Don't ask." Reily filled a water glass at the faucet. "The Quakers think they're Olympians."

Marlin appeared out of nowhere, shaking his hips, ready to dance.

"It's the farm work. Builds muscles." Within the comment, his father delivered a prod, a suggestion that Reily should revisit his agrarian chores.

Reily squatted to pet his canine buddy. "I mowed . . . and I've fed the chickens every day."

His father nodded, in the slow and commanding style that he used with both family and military colleagues. "And I appreciate that, but I want to clean things up for the winter. We need to dismantle the garden, get the rest of the leaves into the compost, and replace and paint boards on the shed and the coop. The last of the corn has to be picked, too."

Reily leaned against the wall to negotiate. "Wil, Boom, and some other friends are coming over today. We're going on a hike." His father inhaled, about to interrupt, but Reily continued, "We scheduled this a while ago."

"Within the past forty-eight hours?"

"Well . . . yes, but it means a lot. Colleen is coming, too." He hadn't yet used her name with Dad.

His father suppressed a smile. "Colleen must be a special lady, taking precedence over important work and all."

"I'll get up first thing tomorrow, and help you all day. Seriously, I already planned to do that."

A too long pause hung with his father, and his graying temples. "Okay, but that's the only thing on the docket tomorrow."

"Yep. You got it."

"Good. Your mother is going to church in the morning. Maybe she'll get your *sister to go with her*." Dad amplified his voice, assuming Rachel might hear and heed the suggestion. "Weather's supposed to be cooperative. We can get a lot accomplished. Today's half-wasted. I didn't get in to Philly from Pensacola until late last evening."

Reily knew his father worked hard. "Thanks, Dad."

"Sure. So who's this Colleen?"

Reily smirked, and sensed a surge of facial color. "You'll see."

Wil promenaded into the Watters's home as if he were the proprietor, carrying a flimsy box. "Mrs. Wiz sends gifts."

"Your mom's the best." Reily reached for a sample. "Hold still."

Reily's father floated into the room, not by coincidence. "Hi Wil, what did your mother make this time?"

"Eclairs . . . the bakery made them this morning." Wil set the goods on the kitchen table.

Mr. Watters extracted a delectable and gnawed, custard sticking to his chin. "She outdid herself."

"Mom's a baking fiend."

Reily knew Dad liked to shoot the breeze with Wil. They would chatter all afternoon if he let them. He caught Wil's attention. "Help me get my stuff together."

Wil cocked his head with telltale sarcasm. "What do you need? It's only a creek jaunt."

Mr. Watters deadpanned, "You'd think he had a date."

In Reily's bedroom, Wil unfolded a map from his pack. "Check this out. It shows the whole valley. The lines are the elevation—the height above sea level."

"Contour lines. We used topographic maps in scouts." Reily located his house and appraised every surrounding feature, consulting the legend as needed. The details fueled a new appreciation for the local forest and the creek that flowed from it. Its extent impressed, but humanity pushed on every border. "What's this?" He pressed his thumb on a hachured blob at the northern edge of the map.

Wil twisted his face in strained observation. "It says quarry. What quarry?"

"I don't think I've ever gone that far."

"Me neither, but I've been really close."

"Side excursion?" Reily visualized their mishmash squad on special patrol.

Wil, too, must have heard the call of the unknown. He puffed his chest. "Change of plans for this afternoon."

Their attention returned to the newfound map.

Reily charged ahead, Colleen close at his heels. She seemed to enjoy the venture so far. Her stunning looks aside, any girl of his had to value the marvels of nature and the inspiration of an afternoon expedition. Behind them, he heard Wil telling Eddie about the trouble with Kelly Bingham and her angry boyfriend. Lulling at the back of the pack were Boom and Cindy Sutherland, beguiled by one another. Marlin scurried between every member of the party, his coat bedraggled from a prior chase.

At the loch, with the pride of a millionaire showing his estate, Reily explained their geographic position relative to township landmarks.

Autumn air carried an organic tincture over the viridian pool, where leaves drifted like Lilliputian rafts headed nowhere. Eddie removed his boots and treaded into the shallow rim, disguising a grimace. Marlin interpreted the act as license to plunge. Reily had never seen his new dog swim, and Marlin did so deftly.

Colleen fumbled for his hand, and, clinging back, he became king of the kingdom, lord of the land. These were his people. Poised on a rock, he spoke. "Let's keep going. There's more to see." The worthy followers agreed, even incorrigible Eddie.

They scrambled upward, leafy parchment crunching underfoot. Colleen squeezed his hand passing the waterfall she liked. Reily paused above it, letting the others catch up.

Colleen tugged on his sleeve. "Nice shirt."

"Thanks, it's an old one." It took a moment for her sarcasm to sink in. "Alright, so I wear it a lot. It's my favorite." He pretended to pout.

"It's very soft." Colleen massaged the flannel fabric, seeking clemency. "Plus, the colors match the surroundings."

Cindy reached their location. Marlin paced around her—pleased he had made another new friend. "I had no idea this was here." Cindy's gawping words were declaration more than conversation. The Mannequin had christened another believer.

Seconds later came Boom, his grin exceeding normal dimensions. "Ahead are the rocks where I saw the snake."

"I don't think we'll see any snakes today," Reily said. "It might be too chilly."

"But there is sunshine. They may want to warm themselves."

"Boom's right, they're cold-blooded." Cindy conveyed corresponding enthusiasm. "This is the time of year they begin to hibernate, but we might get lucky." Through many seasons of swimming, Reily had come to know Cindy, but they had had few conversations. Kind and quiet were her trademarks. In this one outing, he had already heard more of her voice than in all the past years combined.

Wil and Eddie, the laggards, decided to show. Eddie brandished a log as a hiking stick. Wil took out his trusty map. "Where to next, fearless explorers?"

"We're doing a no-kill snake hunt. Boom's our resident herpetologist." Eddie scoffed at Reily's plan. "No kill, no fun."

Wil placed a hand on his oversized friend's shoulder. "Restrain yourself, master snake charmer. Show us your skills."

"Let's go a little further, to the rocks Boom seeks." Reily appreciated Wil's unofficial role as Eddie's tamer. "Wil, isn't there something else we hope to find?"

"Yep, but I cannot tell. It's a surprise." Wil squinted back at Reily, confirming their expeditionary covenant.

Like Boom's prophecy, rocks materialized, dumped by primeval forces into random piles along the streambanks.

Eddie attacked the stones, a lunatic on a pushing, rolling, and flipping mission. Boom joined in, maintaining a safe distance, probing with caution. Cindy offered suggestions on where to search. Marlin pled to join the excavation.

"They're all crazy." Colleen observed the wranglers from an alluring pose on a downed hardwood.

After ten minutes of jumbled mayhem, millipedes and click beetles qualified as the only major finds. With small boulders strewn in all directions, a starved grizzly could have rampaged the site.

Boom, out of breath, wore a nonconforming frown. "No snakes, Reily. I am sorry."

"It's okay. There will be reptiles another day." Reily lured Colleen from her perch. "Wil, wait for us." He yelled to no avail. His impatient friend disappeared at a distant bend in the diminishing creek.

Eddie, dependably noncommunicative, took the secondary lead, snapping branches on a fiendish course.

Reily bantered with his incomparable girl, keeping the others in sight, including a dog overjoyed with wayfaring.

"Is Eddie always such a loner?" Colleen asked. Sensuous eyeliner and the slight gap of her front teeth toyed with his comprehension.

"That's one of many words we could use to describe him. Pigheaded also comes to mind, but he has a good soul. You would be surprised. He's more talkative one-on-one." Reily stopped and clutched Colleen's pleasing bicep. "Did you hear that?"

It arose again, a hollow call traceable to Wil. They hurried ahead.

Eddie intercepted them. "You've got to see this." From his glee, he might have stumbled upon buried gold or a village of topless majorettes.

They scrambled behind the messenger. Before them, lined up shoulder to shoulder, were the other humans and Marlin. Reily and Colleen joined the row, stupified at the great bite missing from the earth.

Wil flagged Reily. "This would be the quarry."

"Yes. It is." Reily felt small, insignificant. Mute air enveloped a cavernous, unworldly wound. Sheer, slick, solid rock plummeted fifty feet into an azure gulf, a hidden gem far, far below. Trepidation came in a sudden wave. He stepped back and drew in a deep, reassuring breath.

A waterborne eruption disrupted the calm until the reverberations rumbled and faded. Eddie shrugged. "Sorry. I threw a rock."

Deference to the manmade, geologic marvel lasted several minutes before the revelers peeled away, one by one.

Homeward bound, Reily retraced their previous steps, veering close to the supposed lair of constrictors, now disarranged. He remained laser-eyed for the prize with Colleen as his assistant. The group, bearing signs of nature intoxication, crept downhill like shy songbirds searching for worms.

Without warning, Boom squeaked—an uttered blend of euphoria and notification. He stooped over an elongated snake, frozen with fear from the congregation of whispering shadows now forming. Boom hesitated. Eddie maneuvered. In milliseconds, a dusky hose enwrapped Knisely's meaty arm, a cunning hand clamped to an angry head. Cindy and Boom bumped skulls scrutinizing the animal and its underside. "It's a black racer," Boom said with a victor's pride.

Eddie held the being for all to view, before lowering it for Marlin, who sniffed and flinched. Eddie turned to Boom and spoke—the first time Reily saw him engage with Boom. A brief conversation addressed the snake's physiological identifiers before Eddie freed the secretive find. It exited in haste for a subterranean hideout.

Reily noted a missing adventurer. "Has anyone seen Wil?" After a unanimous no, he called out to his friend. Eddie added expletives. Moments later, the absentee came their direction, encumbered by an armful of compact, uniform lumber sporting snazzy colored writing.

"The stakes. You found them." Reily relished their removal, but questioned the legality.

Wil dropped the load at his feet. "Damn things were all over the place. Litter in our forest."

The others regarded the cache, unsure of its relevance.

To Reily, it had clear and detestable meaning. "We can't have that, now can we?"

20

Eddie daydreamed to the spasmodic drone of the motor coach as it crawled toward Philadelphia on the infamous West Bethlehem High School art museum field trip. Commuters clogged the expressway, captains of sedans navigating a polluted asphalt river. A pale arm protruded from a Lincoln's lowered window and flung a cup to the graveled shoulder. Beyond the roadway, a real river—the Schuylkill—glided like glass, seeking a getaway from the litterbug, and other city-blind fools.

Upperclassmen mostly filled the seats—luxurious compared to the planks on district buses. Eddie knew the names of a few of the kids, but most were unknown soldiers in the annual assault on the museum. At some point in the three-year tour of duty, every student took part in the epic invasion. Today's unit included Tim from chemistry, Jim from history, and Sheila from homeroom. The remaining classmate he could accurately tag had the body of an Eagles cheerleader and the warmth of a street brick in January . . . the unparalleled and mysterious Rachel Watters.

Flawless, pastel globes occupied her angelic sockets. Golden waves washed partway down the crescent of her spine. Known for solitary studying and an attachment to a baseball stud from Easton, Rachel-finding could have been the next great board game. Sightings were rare. She shunned Eddie as if he had the Spanish Flu, whether within the walls of the Watters's house or the hallways at school. Due to her chronic absence, Eddie often evacuated her from his mind, and pretended Reily had no sister.

From his elevated vantage point, the immensity of the city took hold. Roads ran to the horizons, houses repeated, buildings decayed. Office towers soared with self-importance. Gobs of people buzzed about the built-up beehive, mostly black people—or so his father said.

The museum materialized like a sprawling Greek temple, occupying a high spot over the Ben Franklin Parkway. Smoke plumed from distant stacks, blending with a nasty haze. When the airbrakes disarmed, a chaperone told the students to muster. Eddie disembarked, yawned, and waited for further orders. Tailpipe exhaust competed with the smell of a breakfast griddle from an unknown kitchen. Rachel glimpsed past him, taking in the metropolitan scenery. *Did she just acknowledge me?* He believed to have witnessed a miniature upturn of her extraordinary mouth, paired with a kindhearted squint.

Now alert and attuned to the possibilities of the day, Eddie levitated up each mammoth step and across a courtyard made for gods. Between mighty pillars, he entered the structure and shuddered—before him spread an unconceivable oasis of art.

Senses ignited as he fused with each painting, some hundreds of years old. Larger-than-life characters signified N.C. Wyeth's pieces. Jackson Pollock and Marc Chagall preferred anarchy, each in their own unique form. Monet's stippled magic turned reality into dreams. A Winslow Homer masterpiece took his mind sailing on tumultuous seas, and almost caused a fight when he refused to relinquish the prime viewing post behind a roped barrier.

Eddie sat alone at lunch, contemplating artistic fame. *What matters more—innate talent or continual learning and practice?* Rachel Watters ceased his pondering, entering the café spectacular and solo. He tried not to notice, but her offhand purchase of potato chips and a Tab had movie star quality. She walked on air.

"Care if I sit here?"

My God, she's only four feet away. "No, that's fine."

Rachel commandeered the round table, leaving two seats between them and uncomfortable silence. Finally, she crunched a chip. "What's your favorite?"

"Huh?"

She rolled her eyes. "Which artist?" He felt an encouraging nudge from a foot unseen.

"Um . . . I don't know." Eddie involuntarily twisted and flexed his bulbous neck. "I liked the guy who painted Yellowstone. It said his stuff helped lead to the protection of the park."

"Thomas Moran?"

Eddie burped. "I guess."

"That's gross." Rachel leered, but her scolding contained a tiny thread of amusement. "Moran was part of the Hudson River School. He and his peers all had that ethereal style . . . you know, skies that seem like they should be in the Bible."

"How do you know so much?"

"Remember, my mom's an artist." Rachel circled the bottle top with her fingers as if under hypnosis. Her locks hung like apple and cinnamon wild oats. "She says you're pretty good, too."

"I don't know." Eddie gulped the rest of his soda.

She laughed. "Is that all you say?"

Eddie laughed a little, too. "Sometimes. Are you going off to college next year?" The question bubbled up from within.

"Somewhere." She blew away an annoying hair in her line of sight. "I'm considering NYU and Bard. Maybe Franklin and Marshall. I have to get my applications in."

"I forget what Reily told me. Are you going to major in business?" With her sexy, serious, sometimes sarcastic style, he could see her brokering deals and making things happen.

She delivered another corrective expression. "Art history." She released a deep, humming breath. "It's in my blood, I guess."

"I bet." Silence. "So which painter do *you* like?"

Rachel cocked her head, as if it were an exam question. "Warhol. Andy Warhol. He's an original. I like his audacity."

Eddie liked the way she spoke, flinging big words with hutzpah. "He's the Campbell's Soup and Marilyn Monroe guy, right?"

Rachel nodded, visibly pleased by his escalating knowledge. "He's from Pennsylvania, too. Pittsburgh. Ever been there?"

"No, I haven't been many places." Vacations were a rarity. Dad once took him fishing in Lewes, Delaware, and they visited cousins in Virginia a couple of times. "Most of my travels have been with Wil's family or yours."

"I remember the time you went camping with us in Gettysburg," her voice teased.

He did, too. Spying under the tent fly, he'd seen her in her underwear. "I learned a lot."

They both snickered.

Rachel balled up her chip bag. "We have another hour. Let's get lost in the museum."

The idea sounded truly *magnum opus* . . . whatever that meant.

21

Reily dried his hair and face while pool water puddled at his feet. At the far corner of the natatorium, he caught his mother standing in the doorway, shoulders slumped. He scrambled up to her.

"What are you doing here? It's seven-thirty." She never came to morning practice.

"Your father's on his way to the hospital." His mother pursed her lips. "They think he may have had a heart attack."

The words ricocheted. Reily wobbled and reached for the bench tight to the wall. "What do you mean?"

"I heard him go outside to get the morning paper, and when he came back in, well, I don't know . . . I found him on the sofa, soaked in sweat. He *asked* me to call an ambulance."

Other kids looked on, tuning in to the drama. Reily peered through them, seeing home and the situation described. The consummate do-it-yourselfer, Dad would not have sought help unless things were bad. "Can we go see him?"

His mother flattened her dress, a subliminal sign of confusion and distress. "I'm not sure, but we should try. I'll talk to your coach while you change. We have to get your sister, too."

Mom steered with stoicism. Rachel blubbered in the back seat. Cars clogged Route 22 as if it were any other day, oblivious to the trauma.

The emergency wing of the Allentown Regional Medical Center had a drive-up loop for ambulances. One blocked the lane, disgorging a moaning, elderly man whiter than a department store dummy. Inside, Reily's mother told an admitting nurse why they were there. The plump, so-called caregiver had the warmth of arctic tundra. She directed them to chairs in a noisy waiting area with a Lysol stench. Reily found a recent issue of *Sports Illustrated* with George McGinnis on the cover. The star player of the 76ers reminded him of the time he and Dad went to the Spectrum to see the Harlem Globetrotters. His father had paid extra attention to him on such special occasions. Maybe he hoped to make up for the countless hours spent away from home. At his side or far away, Dad had a positive presence in Reily's life. He knew a friend—and other kids—that couldn't say the same. Meanwhile, his mother stared at the registration counter, rapt in her own thoughts. Rachel continued to sniffle. He wondered what his father might be thinking and feeling, when a different nurse—more congenial than the other—called their last name. Three corridors later, they were ushered into the ICU to find a woozy Keith Watters showing them a signature thumbs-up sign.

If not for the tubes and wires piercing his body, he would have received a proper hug.

Reily accompanied his mother on a return visit to the hospital after spending a chunk of the day fixing a split rail fence and entertaining Marlin, who sensed a change in household regularity. Calls to Colleen and Wil communicated the bad news. Rachel made a strange offer to notify Eddie personally.

Mom navigated doorways and hallways in a sickbay on rest mode. Visitors whispered. Technicians scribbled notes onto charts. Dad, now in his own room, watched a *Green Acres* rerun on a black and white set.

"Move those chocolates, Reily. Let your mother sit there." Dad's gentle demands were a small, but hopeful indicator of recovery started.

Mom leaned over his father. "Keith, what did you learn from the doctors?" She spoke to him as if quizzing an elementary school student.

"I have a partial blockage, but they think the blood thinner is helping. They're scheduling me for angioplasty tomorrow . . . a plumber's coming to unclog me."

"Maybe this will force you to take your blood pressure medicine." Karen Watters could be stern on demand.

Reily told his father about the successful fence repair. His mother said that a juried exhibit had selected one of her paintings. An aide interrupted, shuttling forth a dinner of overcooked chicken and meager sides.

"I'll go to the cafeteria and find real food for me and Reily." Mom popped to her feet and winked at her husband. "Behave yourself and maybe I'll bring you a treat, too. You two can talk about me in my absence."

Keith forced a mischievous smile. "We could be here a while."

Reily took his mother's vacant chair, and listened to her footsteps grow distant. "I didn't know you have high blood pressure."

Dad waved his hand. "It isn't that high. That's why I didn't tell you."

Reily had his doubts. Dad never talked about himself. The greater world, and all its machinations, mattered more, especially international affairs, the state of the nation, and conditions in the immediate community. His loyalty to place could never be questioned.

"What do you think caused the heart attack?" Muttering the lethal words brought a shiver.

"Probably the blockage, the lack of blood flow, but if you mean what might have aggravated things, I'm not sure. I have a few ideas, though." Dad poked at a pasty scoop of mashed potatoes. "I had a rough flight the other day. We moved a plane to Dover and had an incident with the controls. For a few moments, I thought we might crash." His father paused, and stared into nothing. "I thought, this is it, and I knew I'd miss all of you so much." His eyes moistened.

Reily sniffed back tears. "That sounds scary." *I would miss you, too.* Life would be hollow without his father's steady hand and reassurance.

"There's something else I wanted to tell you, and maybe it affected me, too. It sure made me angry."

"What?"

"They filled in Kemp's pond."

Reily froze in disbelief. "Who? When?"

"Monday. I stayed home. I heard noise and walked down to see what was going on. A contractor had equipment there, and had already pushed a bunch of soil into the water by the time I arrived. I let him have it, but it didn't do any good. I figured you would see it soon enough. I didn't have the heart to tell you."

"How can they do that?" Reily wilted in his chair.

"I don't know all the rules about that sort of thing, but it might not be legal." Dad scrunched upwards in the bed, dragging his hookups with him. "It made me sick to see it happen. The man accused me of trespassing and threatened to call the police, so I left. I was tempted to go back and . . . well, enough said."

Reily imagined the scene in his mind and felt short of breath. "Thanks for letting me know." He put his head back in the chair, seeking comfort from a bland ceiling. Dad resumed eating, the fork scraping the plate like heavy equipment grading land into oblivion.

"Do you want this applesauce?" Dad broke the dark reverie.

"I don't have an appetite." Reily bent closer to his father. "Did you really give the guy a hard time?"

Keith Watters hesitated, and then punctuated the air with a butter knife. "I suppose I did. I should have said more, but you do the best you can."

22

Wil escorted Reily on another afterschool pilgrimage to the creek. The gray and disconsolate day matched his best friend's mood. "I'm sorry about your pop."

"Thanks. It's good to have him home again." Reily seemed to be counting the acorns strewn over the ground.

"It feels like forever since we last went fishing. Why did you want to go downstream today?"

"To stay away from Kemp's."

Neither did Wil prefer to see or think or talk about the atrocity at the farm—where he once subdued his biggest bass, a snapping turtle attacked Eddie's shoe, and Reily fell headfirst into a raspberry thicket. He still remembered the scratches and screaming. "This cold's going to make the fish lazy."

"Let's go to the bridge." An undertaker would have muttered with more zest.

"We are. What gives? I think it's more than your dad's health."

Reily attacked a branch in his path. "Everything. Dad. The pond. Now, Colleen. She's acting weird."

Wil jabbed a friendly punch at Reily's shoulder. "Maybe she's menstruating?"

"No, it's something else. Either she's losing interest in me or there's trouble at home. Our calls usually last an hour or longer. Last night she 'had to go' after ten minutes."

"You hook one of those stocked, monster palominos, and your worries will be forgotten. They're top-notch fighters."

"We aren't going to catch anything. I can see my breath." Reily exhaled to accentuate his point.

"Such fatalism. You're going to jinx us."

Reily perked a pinch. "Fatalism—is that a new word you learned in English?"

"Very funny." No one normally tackled life with the same kind of subtle, inner energy as Reily. Gloom infected him about as often as a plague of locusts, but when it did, everyone suffered. "I meant to tell you, and this may not cheer you up: there's a meeting on Wednesday night about the hydroelectric thing."

Reily tripped on a groundhog's hole. "What? Where?"

"The water authority. They have their regular meeting, but according to the paper, they're also voting on the deal to let the reservoir and dam to be built." Wil came to a halt. "The article said that even if the authority approves the project, the company needs other approvals from the state's Department of Environmental Resources. I guess that's the good news."

"All anyone cares about is money." Reily set his fishing rod on the ground. "Hold on. I have to pee." He wetted the base of a silver maple cloaked in seasonal drabness and spoke with his face to the trunk. "We can't let anything happen to the creek."

"You don't have to convince me, but somehow we have to make others get it."

Reily zipped with determination. "We have two days to figure out how."

Say of the Day: discombobulated.

The Mannequin, too, seemed sluggish and mired in despair. The circulation below the bridge's abutments stewed a taciturn, muddy broth. Three miles further, the creek blended with the Lehigh River, its dominant, and often discolored, cousin. Seldom did they go so far, and Wil wasn't taking them there on this strange day—not with Reily in such a hapless condition.

Cars on afternoon errands played the steel, open grates in discordant tones. Wil ignored the four-wheeled interference and, with scant hope of action, regarded his and Reily's descending fishing lines. They waited, waist to railing. Wil reeled a few turns of the handle knowing the smart fish stayed close to cover. "Have you seen Eddie?"

"Every week. Mom's favorite student. That bad boy is pretty gifted, you know?"

"I think he's infatuated with your mom." Karen Watters did have an affable bounce to her step.

"That's disgusting." Reily buttoned the top of his canvas jacket, getting ready for an evening shift at an iron forge or just the family woodstove. "I think you have the wrong Watters woman. He has a soft spot for Rachel."

"I bet it's not soft at all . . ."

"Seriously, he hasn't stopped talking about her since the Philly trip. I guess they bonded."

"He'd like to bond with her alright . . ." Rachel had subtle, taut curves and a likeness to her mother, minus the pleasant personality.

Reily disregarded the quip. "What's up with you, Casanova? No more Kelly episodes, I trust?"

"Hardly." Wil wondered if a recent squeeze fest at Dinardo's qualified for disclosure.

"That's not reassuring. Troy and company will use you as the blocking dummy during football practice. They'll tie *you* to a sled."

Wil reached in his coat pocket for a stashed Milky Way. "Kelly says they're done. Finished."

Reily grabbed at his ropey, seaweed head, deeply panged. "And you'll be finished off. Troxell will blame you for the breakup."

"No worries, Watters." Wil severed a chunk of the candy bar, chewing carefree, tasting sweetness. "You better check that line. Something's bound to bite."

23

The last public meeting Boom experienced involved uniformed military officials with automatic weapons and nefarious political objectives. He assumed tonight's assembly would be safer and far less intimidating than the one in Entebbe two years ago at the Wildife Center. President Amin, the dictator, spoke nonsense as thunder growled over Lake Victoria.

Mr. Kreider called to him before he exited the classroom on his way to meet Cindy. Their regular water fountain rendezvous before lunch marked the most anticipated part of the school day.

"I've been meaning to ask. Did you ever find the snake again?"

Boom appreciated the teacher's interest in his zoological pursuits. "Yes, I should have told you. We verified it was a black racer."

"Nice work. Racers are a fascinating species. They actually pin their prey with their bodies and swallow it whole."

"What kinds of things do they eat?"

Kreider grew animated at the question. "Toads, frogs, insects, small birds and mammals—whatever it can catch."

"I'd like to learn more about snakes. In Uganda, they are often feared, but not so in the United States?"

Kreider shrugged. "I'm not so sure about that. People have an irrational revulsion to them. Most snakes are harmless. There are only three venomous species found in Pennsylvania."

Cindy stood at the doorway. "Timber rattlers, copperheads, and the Eastern massasauga."

"She knows her stuff." Kreider spoke to Boom, but tipped his brainy head at Cindy.

Boom beamed, wide-eyed. "Yes, she helped me find the racer."

"Well, snake hunters, keep investigating. Science needs your inquiry." The teacher pulled down the projection screen, readying for the next class. "Just be careful and respectful, despite the disrespect of others."

In the hall, Boom engaged Cindy during their priceless journey of short minutes. He told her of the public meeting and the inane project—all the information funneled to him from Reily.

"That's terrible." Cindy took on a warrior face. "We can't let them do that."

"Yes, you are right. Would you like to attend with me?"

"Certainly," she said, without hesitation.

He sensed her trust, *her affection*, for him mushrooming like fungi on a receptive tree.

With Dad precluded from driving and Mom guest lecturing for an evening art course at Moravian College, Reily had Rachel shuttle him and his sidekicks to the water authority outpost for the public pow-wow. A virgin meeting goer, Reily feared manipulation and dishonor by aggrandizing adults. He and his car co-occupants, partners in countless journeys past and future, faced a potentially catastrophic realignment—their known existence was in jeopardy should the creek fade away. The changes proposed defied comprehension. One routine but wonderful afternoon, he watched a minnow in a Mannequin pool for minutes on end as it probed and glided, simultaneously innocent and wise, seeking something, anything, everything. But not this fate.

Eddie rode up front, beside Rachel. *How did he get the shotgun seat?* Wil bounced beside Reily on the back seat, the shocks on the Watters's oldest vehicle begging for replacement.

Wil gave him an appraising look. "Are you going to do the talking . . . assuming we get a chance?"

"You're the one with the facts."

"But you're the poet—our unsanctioned orator."

Eddie cracked up and spun around. "The hippie spokesman. They're going to love us."

Rachel chastised Reily through the rearview mirror. "Don't make a fool of yourself."

"I plan not to, but worse things could happen." Reily hated the pressure, but a defenseless creek and forest required his voice. They spoke in their own language, but too few listened. Wil had talked him and the others into attending. For whatever reason, it seemed natural to go—a normal thing for a concerned kid.

The car rumbled into the last space on a smooth and meticulous lot. Windows of the building blazed like an alien insurrection. Inside, aging humans—supportive, curious, or apprehensive—occupied rows of portable chairs. Two youthful outliers—one ebony, the other ivory—signaled from the other side of the room. Boom gave an OK sign. Cindy sat, shoulders back, ready for anything.

Reily scanned the place for a bathroom, in case the meeting turned endless. Beside him, Wil pulled out a notebook, serious about his journalism. Eddie whispered a secretive comment to Rachel, hyper-fancy in a dress and heels. She employed the seat at the end the row, already prepped for exit.

The five-man water authority board spoke hushed to one another, strategizing for battle or, ideally, retreat. At the top of the hour, all rose as if the seats had automatic lifts, and bumbled the pledge of allegiance. The board member in the middle of the pack ambled to a podium and thanked the audience for being there. His introductory speech tumbled into a confession about the main purpose for the evening party, namely, premeditated ecological murder.

Next up, the mastermind of the madness, a Mr. Darkes, came forward preparing for a commencement address.

"It's good to see so much interest in our forward-thinking project."

Reily boiled at the words. The greasy man had skinny limbs, slimy hair, and a bulbous belly. A shrewd voice droned beneath reading glasses sliding down a crooked nose.

"Clean, safe hydroelectric power promises to keep electricity affordable and create American energy independence." Darkes paused for scattered applause. "Imagine a sparkling lake, recreational opportunities, and Pennsylvania pride in powering our economy, and improving the quality of life. There are no downsides."

A slide projector illuminated a screen beside the declaimer of doom, and drawings appeared, then artist renderings of a mock utopia. Numbers followed in charts and graphs, with more talk of improvements and lower taxes enabled by the deal.

Eddie looked at Reily and mimed a finger down his throat. Reily wanted to gag. *What about the wildlife and the forest?* He recalled more Mannequin memories. A morning walk sparked a five-year-old's astonishment, every sense wide-open under his father's guiding hand. Beech buds doubled as miniaturized spears. A hollow branch became an imaginary canoe for Playskool people. A rug of hemlock needles, thick and bouncy, trickled their spiced fragrance.

The charlatan's propaganda ceased. "So what questions do you have for me? Eastern Power wants to set you at ease."

The crowd vibrated. Arms poked upwards. The lead-off board member selected interrogators one by one, but the questions were pathetic.

"What's it going to do for the fishing?"

"How much did you say our taxes will go down?"

"Will dogs still be allowed on the land?"

Reily wanted to scream, but instead he stood. An involuntary reflex. All eyes were on him—the sap without a prepared speech. "My name is Reily Watters. I attend West Bethlehem High School—"

"That's nice, son," the chief board member cut in, "but you didn't raise your hand. You'll have to wait your turn."

A few people laughed . . . before Cindy rose to her feet. "Sir, my classmate has a right to speak."

Board members murmured to their appointed leader. The leader cleared his throat. "Alright, please proceed, young man, but I ask folks to please wait their turn." Mr. Darkes rocked on his toes, agitated.

Reily let it flow. "I live near the Mannequin Creek and I have spent many days enjoying it. I can tell you, it is a true wonder . . . a park without being a park, a wildlife refuge but not called one. There are waterfalls, swimming holes, trout, and all kinds of plants and animals. How many of you have been there?"

A sea of arms reached upwards. The authority honcho stiffened. Mr. Darkes straightened his tie.

"Then you know we shouldn't mess it up." Sympathetic clapping whirred through the ether. Reily could think of nothing else to say. He returned to the safety of seated companions, drained from his brief but necessary rhetoric.

Other questioners and commentators took their turns. Wil scrawled notes. Board members watched the clock. The room grew restless with coughs, yawns, and shifting bottoms until the leader dismissed Mr. Darkes and broke the news: the board would meet in private to make a decision.

"This sucks," Eddie repeated, over an ABBA song on the radio.

Wil tucked his pen beneath his mop and over an ear. "It shouldn't be allowed."

Reily wondered how fast the authority would render a verdict.

Eddie popped his fat cranium over the headrest. "I can't believe Boom and what's-her-name came together."

"You mean Cindy?" Reily tuned in. "Why would you say that?"

Rachel glanced at Eddie. "Yeah, what's wrong with it?"

Eddie shrunk. "Just saying . . . he's black. She's white."

"Really?" Rachel enlisted her gift of mockery. "Wil? Reily? Did you know Boom is black?"

"That's news to me. I thought he was chestnut or mahogany." Wil slid his hands over the seat to jab at Eddie. "You are darned observant, Knisely."

Rachel scowled an unspoken reprimand at her front seat passenger. If Reily knew his sister, Eddie's punishment had only begun.

24

Why must I have so much homework? Boom's friends were experiencing the real-life geometry of basketball while he memorized the properties of isosceles, equilateral, and right triangles. He answered the final math question and pushed the textbook aside.

Next up, biology. Tomorrow's quiz would cover the principles of ecology. Mr. Kreider provided the definitions. Boom had to match them with the proper term. He reviewed the concepts of symbiosis and commensalism. *Which one applied to his relationship with Cindy?* Maybe mutualism better defined their interactions. Oh, how they benefitted one another . . . and he certainly appreciated her phenotype.

Thirty-five minutes later, his father dropped him curbside at the entrance to Weyant Park. Boom wore two sweatshirts, a knit hat, and tight-fitting gloves to defend himself from the cold. The crest of the hill glowed under coin-operated court lights. He hoped Reily and Wil were still there.

Wil watched Reily miss another shot. "You're trying to muscle it. Remember, it's all in the wrist."

"I'm done. It's not my night." Reily chased down the ball and slunk to the bench.

Wil joined him. "It's never your night when you're playing me."

Reily shut out the comment behind bangs that hung like a curtain.

"What gives? Are you still having issues with your lady?"

"Colleen's acting even weirder. She avoided me today at school."

"You're imagining things."

"No, she turned around when she saw me."

Wil considered the situation. "Maybe she thinks you have your eyes on someone else?"

"Who? There's no one else . . . and she knows that."

"Maybe . . ." Wil spotted three silhouettes making their direction from the east side. "I think we're going to have company."

Reily lifted his head. "Oh crap. Is that Troy, as in Kelly's Troy?"

Wil needed no further confirmation. "We better get out of here. Fast."

Reily led a disguised escape attempt, but their brisk pace gave it away.

"Come back here, you pussies!" The angry growl matched the voice of a rogue fullback.

Wil's legs discovered urgency. With survival as stimulus, he commenced an unplanned, downhill sprint, passing Reily and testing the hustle of the high school's leading rusher.

"Go, go." Reily's heavy feet thumped the ground.

A taunting yell from the hilltop. Aborted pursuit. Temporary safety. Wil slowed. "We can stop now."

Boom tromped up the main path. To his left, a row house released a smoky plume, heralding winter's approach. A cacophony of voices disturbed his contemplations. The court came into view, occupied by fellow teens.

"How's it going?" Boom saw neither of his friends. Maybe they were late, too. The three boys in front of him scoffed. They were vaguely familiar and visibly agitated.

"You're a friend of Wisnoski's, aren't you?" The largest member of the group spoke, studying Boom as if he were a loathed insect. The disproportioned boy had a pointed face, like that of a ferret or mink.

Boom hesitated, remembering Wil's last name. "Yes, I know Wil. I am supposed to meet him here."

"That so. What do you guys think?" The half-human, half-mustelid turned to his companion carnivores, one short and round like a predatory

snail, the other slender, with a distended lower jaw—an upland barracuda. "What are the chances of chickenshit Wisnoski or goofball Watters
showing up now?"

The snail slid closer. "They're cowards. We need to show them con-
sequences, Troy."

Without further instruction, the animals encircled Boom. "May I ask
what my friends did to upset you?"

The barracuda opened its mouth. "None of your business." A second
later, the fish-kid flicked his head, a primal signal, and the massive ferret
tackled Boom without warning.

Boom bounced hard, his head careening off the macadam. A high-top
sneaker kicked his stomach, leaving him gasping for breath. Repetitive
fists pummeled his eyes, cheeks, and nose. Pain blurred his consciousness. Deadweight crushed his thigh until he heard a faraway declaration:
"Let's get out of here."

25

Out the bedroom window, snowflakes tumbled out of the sky like intricate origami. Each inch of accumulation increased the likelihood Colleen would have a second day off school—guaranteed boredom, but shelter from Reily's annoying, yet endearing, persistence. She ran her fingers across the creek rock he had given her, heavy and round, the color of a bad thunderstorm. He told her it would *lift* her spirits.

Bad news compounded every day. First, the senior jocks messing with Boom. Now, her mom's secretive plans to move. Colleen curled up and turned on the radio. Music usually made her feel better.

A sad song by America added gray to her outlook. *Ohio? Why Ohio?* No beaches. No mountains. Days would drag on, one by one, like never-ending rows of corn. Proof lacked that her mother intended to take them to farm country, but they had relatives in the Buckeye State and Mom was born there. Colleen thought she'd heard her say Bishopsville during a cagey phone conversation. On a map, Colleen found a town by the same name close to Athens, Ohio, where Cousin Donna lived. Mom often complained about her job and talked of trying something new. Colleen feared that day had finally come.

By noon, she mustered energy to search for a snack. Under the overhead light, the phone on the kitchen wall tempted her. *No. We need to make space between us.* Making space. What did that mean? She had few friends except guys who lusted for her. Other girls were jealous. She wasn't a jock or brainiac, but she did okay at sports and could get good grades if she tried harder. Colleen Mills . . . even her name sounded ordinary.

Lovers conspired on a soap opera. The characters, perfect and pretty, resigned themselves to a painful breakup. Pretzels crunched all the same, but the bland flavor brought an epiphany: they tasted better when she hung out with Reily.

A washcloth swabbed Reily's face. He reached out, but the washer eluded him. He tried again, grasping at nothing, and awoke. Marlin panted with guilt beside him. Reily remembered his mother mentioning a second round of snow. He had fallen back to sleep.

Sullen light slipped into the space. He lifted his head to confirm the presence of an outside world. Nearly a foot of pristine fluff coated every horizontal surface, including those with modest slope. Geometry had meaning after all.

He rummaged for clothing, suitably warm and amply worn, while Marlin claimed territory on the bed. Sure as sunrise, the dog's pseudo nap would end when Reily left the room.

The day necessitated wool socks and a certain flannel shirt. He imagined Colleen commenting on his clothing choice. They could spend the afternoon together, but she had not made contact for *three days*. Come evening, he would try calling her . . . again.

Boom deserved a call, too. And a heartfelt apology.

In the kitchen, cooling pancakes waited on a plate. A sneeze from the studio proved Mom's proximity.

"You're up, finally?" His mother appeared, overdressed for a dim, dull day. "Heat those up. Have a banana, too. They're getting ripe."

"Yes, Mom." He checked for coffee. A warm pot contained a residual cup or two.

"That's not good for you, you know."

From the cabinet, Reily retrieved a favorite mug adorned with pine trees and a wavy streak of navy blue suggesting a stream. "I need something to wake me up."

"Your father's working from the desk in our room. He wants you to feed the chickens."

"How is he feeling?"

She hesitated in response. "Not a hundred percent. It will take time."

Reily scratched the fuzzy head pushing against his thigh. "Marlin will help with the feeding. He loves the chickens."

His mother frowned slyly. "Don't let him chase them."

The phone rang, startling them both.

Reily answered. "Hello?"

"Did you see all the snow?" Wil had a knack for the obvious.

"Hard to miss. I am thinking sledding, maybe three o'clock. I have stuff to do around here first."

"The day's a-wasting, Watters."

"Right, Mr. Rise and Shine Punctuality."

"I heard something distressing, by the way." Wil disbursed discouraging information in matter-of-fact spurts. He would make a terrible doctor.

"What now? Did Troy beat up somebody else?"

"The water authority dummies approved the big project."

Pancake braked in Reily's esophagus. "As in a huge lake and dam?"

"Unfortunately. One of the mechanics who works for my dad is tight with one of the board members. The formal announcement happens next week."

The idea of sledding became uneventful, feeding chickens a heavy-weight chore. "Why do people have to screw things up all the time?"

Wil turned silent for a second. "I'm an independent thinker, or so my mother says, but pastor what's-his-name once said, 'people are broken'—and he didn't mean in a compound fracture kind of way."

Wil had a way with words. This time they failed to provide comfort.

26

The turkey carcass took the form of a vulture. The mashed potatoes hyperbolized his recent humiliation. Other suitable terms included smashed, pounded, and pulverized.

"You must eat, Boom." His mother, calm and petite, offered him the bowl of corn.

He shook his head. Speaking required too much effort.

"Son, you need to cheer up. Your wounds are healing well, so must your outlook." His father's viewpoint always carried depth and meaning.

Boom understood and agreed, but felt far from thankful this Thanksgiving day. Fitting in with eastern Pennsylvania hadn't been easy. Now, word had spread about last Thursday's fight—an *attack*, unprovoked and unwarranted. People would assume the black kid, the Negro from Africa, somehow caused the trouble.

"Would it help if we looked at other schools?"

"Are you crazy, Mom? I have friends at school."

"At the least, I think you should talk to the police." His mother wiped her mouth with one of the fancy cloth napkins only used on holidays. "They need to know what those boys did to you."

Boom tasted the stuffing. The scab on his lip accepted the mild seasoning. "They will not believe me and they certainly won't discipline the football team's most famous athlete."

His father drank wine from a silver chalice, another sign of the holidays. With a sensitive but serious expression, he tipped his glass. "Justice only prevails when it is sought."

The statement hung in the air, floating for consideration, while they dispensed and digested the remainder of the meal.

Eddie sliced himself another piece of ham. "How come we're not having turkey?"

"You make it, we can have it." His father spoke from a recliner facing the primordial television with a grimy screen. The Packers were playing the Eagles. "Don't eat all the food. I can use it for lunches."

Compared to the pilgrim day feasts in other households, the Knisleys came in last place. Their piss-poor lineup: instant stuffing, buttered lima beans, jellied cranberry, and a slab of smoked pig. The food surpassed their crappy rating for family bonding. His older brothers were gone as usual, one at a girlfriend's house, the other working or smoking pot.

Eddie made a face on his plate, using the beans for eyes and a smeared portion of cranberry sauce for a mouth. Fragments of ham became eyebrows and a nose, while his father yelled at the set.

"They pay these monkeys enough. You'd think they'd be able find the end zone."

Eddie visualized chimps scurrying around the backfield, but he knew the real meaning of the commentary. He watched a replay of the failed play. "The white dude missed the block on the end."

His father half-rotated in the chair. "James could have broken outside. He's lazy. Coach needs to motivate him." Dad resumed his NFL trance. "More watermelons in his locker." The bigot's shoulders quivered as he humored himself.

Eddie took his dirty plates to the sink and wrapped foil over the leftovers, jamming them into the fridge beside a gallon of expired milk. "I'm heading to Reily's house."

"Alright." The response came delayed and distant.

Daylight vanished as Eddie pedaled away from his dismal house and its rotting siding. He wanted to see Rachel more than Reily, but both were in Maryland, with aunts and uncles, doing what real families do on holidays. Options were limited. Wil's mom had banned him from the Wisnoski house for eating an entire cookie order. Friends were scarce. Boom came to mind, but who knew if he wanted to do anything? They had yet to hang out together. The football goons had done a number on him. *What a shitty move.* Eddie rode in circles on cindered, slushy

pavement, deep in thought, until seduced by a most righteous notion. He nosed his bike onto Center Street and beelined north, skirting piles of filthy roadside snow. Duty called.

Eddie cruised in temporary ecstasy, ignoring the sting of icy winter air. He had found direction. A pat on his right thigh confirmed a certain object. *Don't leave home without it.*

27

Merle Darkes served his mother another helping of her inglorious holiday gelatin salad—Thanksgiving leftovers which she consumed posthaste, fragments of pineapple dangling from her lips. Those lips were neither capable of sustaining logical, interesting conversation, nor had they ever uttered much in the way of encouraging, nurturing dialogue.

She had been with Merle since Wednesday, physically but not mentally. During a business call, she barged into his home office demanding to know which dinner seating he had selected for the cruise. Another time, with her swirled wig askew, she asked about the midnight buffet. The only voyage he had coordinated involved a series of doctor appointments via the geriatric shuttle van.

Renewed planning for the Mannequin project tempered the doldrums of maternal overload. According to a confidant, the authority had reached a decision providing Merle and his partners needed assurance. After they resurveyed the site and set new stakes, in as little as forty months, money would gush from four impulse turbines harnessing cool, clean Pennsylvania H2O. He channeled gratefulness to the malleable municipal minions who supported his plans, until Mother passed gas on the opposite side of the table.

The putrid vapor ruined a rekindled appetite, undaunted by the piteous flavor of reheated poultry. Merle, never satiated, yearned for the hedonism of aged beef—prime-cut, restaurant extravagance made accessible by entrepreneurial prowess.

28

Wil stood over his father in the Wisnoski's cramped garage after returning from another weeknight study session at the library. Dad extended a hand from his horizontal position on the creeper.

"Give me that lug wrench."

Wil obliged. "Don't you get tired of working on cars?"

Dad paused, as if the thought had never crossed his mind. "You'd think so, wouldn't you?" He returned to the underside of the '55 MG, the never-ending project. "What's this I hear about your black friend getting in a fight at the park?"

"Do you have to describe him by his skin color? Who told you about a fight?"

"I have my sources." Dad groaned, and cursed at the car. The wrench clanked on the concrete. "I also heard someone cut the valves on the back tires of Troy Troxell's Plymouth." Dad reemerged. "What's the story?"

The revelation caught Wil off guard. "Beats me." Things began to make sense. Reily said that Troy passed him in the hall and ran a finger across his throat in a slicing motion. Wil assumed the loathing had to be associated with his getaway at Weyant Park and the proclivities of a certain girl.

"Your friend didn't vandalize Troy's car?" Dad stared, slick-haired, expecting an honest answer.

"No way. Boom is a good person. He wouldn't do that." Wil believed his own words, *but if not Boom, who?* Then it struck him: *Kelly must have another sucker on her stringer.*

His father plucked a menthol Winston from a chest pocket, sat up, and snapped a lighter. A cloud rose. "Why'd they mess with . . . what's his name?"

"Boom." Wil fiddled with the car's antique headlight. "Me and Reily were shooting hoops, and Troy and his football buddies showed up and went after us. We got away, but Boom had come looking for us and ran into them."

"You two left him there?"

"We didn't know it happened. We were long gone."

The elder Wisnoski tapped cigarette ashes into a coffee can filled with butts. "I hope you apologized to Boom." A question obscured as a comment.

Wil studied the oil marks on the ground. "Yeah, I did. I felt bad about what happened."

"I need that piece of hose on the bench."

Dad caught his eye on the handoff. "Are you sure you and Reily didn't take revenge on the big, bad bully?"

"No, I swear." Wil's voice cracked from the tension.

"I believe you." Dad rolled out of view, except for his scuffed work shoes. "Only thing I can't figure out is why they wanted to go after you. You never had any trouble with Troy before."

Wil froze. "I don't know . . ."

"Just a guess, but I bet there's a girl involved."

Wil had no response.

"Be careful, son. Love makes people weird."

Wil glanced at the Snap-on Tools calendar. The bikini babe stared back like a wanton Kelly with fewer clothes. "Thanks for the kind advice."

Say of the Day: interrogation.

29

"We used to fish right here." Reily kicked at the ground with the heel of his hiking boot, hoping ghost sunfish would forever bite the soles of clueless homebuyers.

Without buildings or fencerows, the compacted acres lacked reference. Farm reduced to wasteland. A swath of bare, frozen earth approximated the spot where a snapping turtle once chased Eddie and a baby muskrat burrowed into Wil's knapsack. The buried pond would soon be a forgotten relic under a future road or lot in Kemp Manor to come.

"This is wrong." Boom sounded inordinately indignant for someone who had never enjoyed the place.

"Yes, very wrong." Reily peered across the sloping grade toward the Mannequin Valley and a plot of forsaken evergreens—dollops of color amidst December bleakness. "We have to pick one of those, cut the top off, and carry it back to my house."

"No worries. What is the saying . . . piece of cake?" Despite fresh scars from the assault at Weyant Park, Boom's positivity never waned.

Reily welcomed the crisp air against his cheeks as they trudged downhill. The cold planet smelled vacant, sterilized. "How are you feeling? Those imbeciles aren't giving you any more trouble, are they?"

"No. I don't think they will bother me anymore."

How can you be so sure? "Derelict Troy gave me a blind side shove into a locker this week."

"It will stop soon. They know they were wrong." Boom stooped in carefree wonder to study a gray blob on a stem. "What is this?"

"It's an ootheca—the egg case of a praying mantis." Reily had a sudden notion. *Maybe Boom did the number on Troy's tires.*

"I guess it belonged to an insect. It looks like hard foam." Boom returned upright. "Good construction."

No way. Boom wouldn't hurt a person, or a tire. "Yep. Solid. Better than the houses they're going to build here."

Where the land flattened, they evaluated pine after pine. Reily halted at a tall tree with lush foliage and conical perfection. "Right shape, perfect size."

Boom displayed his showy enamel. "It is as if you are describing Colleen."

"Ha. She doesn't like to talk to me much anymore."

"That will change, my friend." Boom reached for the conifer's trunk. "You see, here, it is quite thin, like Cindy."

"You're too funny." Reily sized up the saw. "Time to lay Cindy down."

Seismic laughter, big and melodic, reverberated across the township.

Reily climbed, one branch at a time, sap sticking to his gloves. He peered downward and shuddered—the ground, and Boom, waited fifteen feet below. He had a flashback to the fall at the pool. His grip tightened.

With one hand, he sawed. Metal teeth chewed through the four-inch trunk in minutes. The uppermost fourth of the tree tipped without complaint, and tumbled, bouncing upon impact. Reily felt a tinge of remorse for the portion truncated, no longer able to volunteer seed and cover to animals in need.

Back on terra firma, Reily hoisted the piece of the tree on his shoulder. Boom handled the pointy end. The sun tussled with rangy clouds, brightening the schlep. Determination wrestled doubt. The forested grotto upstream, another potential site of land abuse, deserved every ounce of fortitude they could muster. Marlin barreled his way and carried a kennel's worth of courage.

Reily massaged the dog's warm ears with his free hand. "Who let you out?" Marlin barked a secret answer.

The spirit of the season—and seasons to come—seemed mired. A long, lonely winter awaited if the Colleen crisis remained uncorrected. Spring and summer would never be the same if the dam and hydro thing proceeded.

At least he had his friends . . . and the world's coolest canine, leading them home, upbeat and unfazed.

30

"What is this?" Rachel arched her eyebrows at the wrapped package.

Eddie nudged it toward her. "A present." The lamp in the Watters's living room backlit his hunny. She glimmered like a diamond.

"The bow sort of gave that away." Rachel cast a wry look. "Why are you giving me a Christmas gift?"

A skintight sweater stuck to her body, making up for the lack of appreciation. If only he could decode her strange communications.

"Open it." He kept his distance, acknowledging her rank. Rachel controlled the relationship.

She showed another indecipherable facial expression before her sleek hands pulled at the ribbon. Paper fell away from a flat box. She parted the cardboard with a tug and withdrew a stout book, H.W. Janson's *History of Art*.

Eddie studied her reaction. "Me and Reily found it at the bookstore in town."

Rachel remained stoic and leafed through several pages. "You mean *Reily and I*." She stopped at a European classic of a nude woman reclining on an elegant loveseat. "Is this why you bought it?"

Eddie flushed and straightened. "No. I thought you'd like *all* the stuff in there."

"They're called paintings, Edward." She finally broke a smile.

Rachel moved the book to the antique coffee table before them and scooched closer on the sofa. He inhaled perfume, and wished he could eat the air.

"You deserve a gift, too." She gazed forward, as if considering the merits. "In spite of being a tire cutter."

"What?" Eddie drew an exasperated breath. "What are you talking about?"

"Really? You don't think I know? I figured it out." She pushed scrumptious flaxen hair behind her ear. "You can't get anything past me."

Eddie slumped back and rested his hands behind his guilty head. "Troy asked for it." Smug satisfaction met slivers of remorse. He did not relish the role of vigilante, but some circumstances required a necessary question: *What would Dirty Harry do?* "I thought about Boom . . . the guy's minding his own business and those idiots—led by the idiot-in-chief—beat him up." Eddie chewed on his lip. "It's not right."

Without warning, Rachel placed her hand on his thigh and squeezed. "Good job, Edward." She lightened her enthralling grip. "Seriously, that fool needs his *ego* deflated. He grabbed my butt in tenth grade."

"What did you do?" Eddie punched his palm. "I should drain his tires again."

"Oh, don't worry, he only did it once. I elbowed him in the nuts."

"I see." Eddie squirmed. Rachel defined "feisty" in his dictionary . . . if he actually owned one.

"Close your eyes and put your hand out."

He obeyed.

Soft fingers positioned a cool, heavy object. "Open them."

A veneered wooden handle protruded from a leather sheath. A tiny note card dangled from a green string, reading *Merry Christmas, Big Eddie.* Rachel's swirly signature proved its authenticity. Eddie extracted a seven-inch buck knife, awed in every way. The blade glistened. He searched for the right words. "It's incredible." *Oh no, I sound like a pyscho.*

"I'm glad you like it." Her voice overflowed with unfamiliar sincerity. She pressed into him, breasts against bicep. "Do me one favor," she whispered.

"Okay, what?"

"Use *that* the next time Troy's car needs fixing."

31

Wil rubbed his hands together, stimulating circulation. "What possessed you to want to hike to the quarry the day after Christmas? It's pretty far, you know."

"I had to get outside. I've done nothing but eat the last two days." Reily did seem rounder, but a puffy jacket could have been the source of sudden corpulence. "Eddie was at the house last night, but he barely said hi. Rachel has him cuckoo for Cocoa Puffs."

Wil struggled to keep up with Reily, the human equivalent of a leggy deer amped on coffee. "Ah, the new and improved Eddie. Who should we be more worried about, him or your sister?"

Reily stopped and scanned, enshrouded in misty breath. "Fair question. They *are* the original odd couple. She would kill me for even using the word 'couple.'" Reily took a few crunchy steps. "Who knows, they might kill each other."

An inch of snow, melted and refrozen, mottled the ground like crumbling cement. Marlin skidded where the mess had devolved to icy slicks. Difficulty energized him—dog and master cut from the same cloth.

Wind arrived, stirring the woods and mixing brittle leaves. Stride after stride, Wil's feet beat on rigid ground, land turned impenetrable. The journey along the Mannequin proceeded—ascending, leveling, and rising again. The creek, in a seasonal coma, had nothing to say.

He kicked a rock and watched it skate across the surface. "I hate when the creek's solid. The fish are teasing me."

"Teaching you the virtue of patience."

"The same thing Colleen's instructing?"

Reily raised a hiking stick as a mock weapon. "Stop." The stick, scavenged in the first hundred feet of the day's outing, was scaled with fungus, calling into question its ability to inflict serious pain. He lowered the ailing weapon. "I need to clear my head. She's all I've thought about."

"Did you give her a Christmas present?"

"Sort of." Reily adjusted his knit hat, hair spilling out everywhere. Serpico without the beard. "She agreed to come over on New Year's Eve. I'm taking her to Mixon's Grill for dinner."

"You must be rich. Are you going to propose?" Wil sized another rock to mimic a hockey puck. "I thought we were having a funeral pyre bonfire?"

"We are. She's invited." Reily scrunched his face, eyebrows up, half-smiling—the universal expression of conditional optimism.

"Maybe I should invite Kelly?" Wil yanked down on his own hat, his hair a close second place to Reily's in the race for unruliness.

"Sure . . . if you have a death wish. We could take care of business right then. Barbecue Wil in a gesture of compassion to eliminate future pain and suffering."

"Very funny. Have it your way. I can go solo, observe the mating rituals, and write about them in the Junior High news." Wil framed an imaginary headline. "Winter Romance Tips from Reily Watters."

Reily used his hiking stick as a golf club, driving shards of snow toward Wil. Marlin came to life, captivated by a new game surely designed for his amusement. Another swing followed.

Wil deflected the largest chunks. "Save your energy, lover boy."

Onward. Silence in unison. Peace prevailing. Trees in every direction of every size imaginable. Repetitious yet unique. If one paused long enough to enjoy it, the forest became a shrine for contemplation. A poem from Emerson came to mind, a forced assignment but memorable nonetheless. A writer had to read aggressively to improve.

"Words are coffee for the intellect."

Reily laughed. "Where did that come from?"

"I just made it up, but it is so true. Hey, what ever happened with your poem? Did Colleen like it?"

"I forgot all about it. That was months ago." Reily put the hiking stick over his shoulders, holding it with both hands. "I never gave it to her."

"What? Why not?"

"It sounded dumb."

"No such thing as a bad poem." Reily often verbalized the greatest descriptions and made the kookiest, coolest observations. If fate had Wil writing books one day, an embellished Reily would make a superb character, but not even Hunter Thompson or John Steinbeck could capture all of Watters's idiosyncrasies.

Reily dithered. "Something else has been bothering me."

"Wondering what Eddie did with the magazines, I bet. I have theories, don't worry."

Reily hung his head. "I'm not good at anything."

"Swimmer, angler, outdoorsman, resident soothsayer, stud in the eyes of women." Wil guessed levity might help.

"You're quite the comedian. Seriously, you're the all-star angler, not me, and you're the one sinking sixteen points a game."

"Actually seventeen, but go on."

"I mean it. Basketball. Fishing. You're a natural—even with the ladies. Your swimming isn't bad either, or your writing. Someday, you'll write books, or articles for magazines. My swimming days are fading. My times are lousy. I need to find something else . . . something I can do half as well as the way you do things."

The revelations were new territory. Wil never experienced such candidness from his steady-state friend. Reily could be temporarily glum, but he typically rebounded faster than Julius Erving. "Look, if it makes you feel better, let it be known that I'm a nervous mess when Kelly tries to swap spit. Also, for the record, on many a day *you* are the better fisherman. And one last point, I gave up on swimming because I don't come close to your hydro-dynamism."

"Hydro-dynamism?"

"Never mind. I'm just saying that you have a ton of talent and more awaiting discovery. Do you remember the day you hit every shot in Around the World? Every one, consecutively, for two rounds. *Never* have I done that."

Reily shrugged. "Freak luck, that's all."

"Time froze. The atomic clock stopped."

"We're going to freeze if we don't keep moving." A semblance of happiness seemed to return to Reily. "We have to be close."

"Maybe a few hundred yards that-a-way."

Reily veered. Marlin surveyed for fleeting scents. Cold boots shuffled until the earth opened.

"Would you look at that?" Wil reveled at the scene.

Reily stumbled backwards. "Whoa, Marlin. Be careful." Reily had the hiking stick behind his head again, like Jesus carrying a cross. "It seems bigger, I swear."

The walls of rock glowed at Wil. "I read somewhere that the Lehigh Valley accounted for about half the slate produced in the United States. It was one of the greatest slate-producing regions in the world." Some of his own ancestors had made a risky living working in similar quarries over a century ago.

"Mightily impressive." Reily bore the gaze of a determined messiah seeing God knows what. "It's dangerous, but exquisite. Our own lake."

"A mini ocean. Probably as deep as one." A miserable fact burrowed into Wil's mind. "But this could all change."

Reily maintained the fiery, faraway eyes. "*We're* the arbiters of *this* wilderness."

Axiom. Proverb. The gospel according to Watters.

Say of the Day: clairvoyance.

32

Holidays obliterated productivity. So did televised football. Merle's alma mater appeared constipated against the bulwark of the Crimson Tide defense—the front four as obstinate as an office full of bureaucrats. Penn State's mediocrity tainted the gift he gave himself at Christmas: the mother of all landscape paintings. Spanning sixty inches, the framed depiction of compatible hills and dales mollified the inborn tension between scenery and dominion. A local female artist rendered the piece, but his mother failed to be impressed. She called it uninteresting. This, from a woman who bought Rockwell posters from Gimbels.

Merle checked the pork and sauerkraut in the slow cooker, releasing a puff of sweet, acidic steam. Tomorrow, come noon, he would indulge in an insular, unmemorable feast of one, ushering forth another year of tedium and obscurity.

Beyond the living room's sliding door, graphite clouds marshaled outside in a menacing array, akin to the forces that worked against him day after day. Free enterprise—and the undervalued talents of engineers—built America, but society had gone soft on invention. Rights for this and that bludgeoned the betterment of all, certainly the virtuous acquisition of wealth. Someone had to calm the socialistic headwinds and resurrect founding maxims.

A tarpaulin, stretched and sagging from seized snow and rain, disguised his sacred swimming pool. He pictured chemically improved water against a perimeter of concrete, cheery and bright in summer sunshine less than six months away. The vision induced a modicum of tranquility, transitory at best. A sudden, inflammatory gust of wind arrived, tumbling a favored chair into the stagnant puddle.

Ineffective pool covers were the least of his worries. Assuming Pennsylvania regulators gave Eastern Power the go-ahead in the coming months, the Federal Power Commission had the final word. No license, no hydro project. Benefits had to outweigh costs by Washington math. Merle had to simplify the ratio, solve the equation, in unequivocal terms.

He had to show the advantage, the *rewards* . . . that only water could unleash. Could he do it?

A recent day of skiing in the Poconos piled on self-doubt. Myerhoff, the persuasive sales manager for a turbine manufacturer, slalomed like an alpine pro. "Competence on the slopes builds competence in business," he lectured, a minute before Merle lost a pole on a black run he had been induced to attempt. After a jarring collision, he felt awkward gratitude toward a large tree that had prevented a deathly descent.

He had yet to master his pastimes or his profession.

33

Colleen brushed her hair hoping an extraordinary New Year's Eve dinner would ease her mind. The blow dryer continued to trip the breaker. The curling iron never warmed. The short-term hassles paled in comparison to her long-term predicament. New friends could be made, grades improved . . . *but what about Reily?*

She pilfered mascara from a bathroom drawer full of castaway cosmetics, expiration unknown, and tested lipstick a shade too pink. It would have to do.

For the occasion, she borrowed, from her mother, a dress never worn. Dark blue and knee-length, the material conformed and shimmered for the night's unprecedented formality.

Her purse had room for money, but she had none. After the run-around Reily had endured, she should foot the bill. The fancy restaurant likely came with a crowd of snobby people—tolerable as long as the food matched the hype.

She stuffed faded jeans, dingy earth shoes, and a thick sweater into a souvenir bag advertising Hershey's bars and placed it next to an elongated present, unevenly wrapped, leaning against the wall. Balancing in glossy heels, the contrast in wardrobes instigated a laugh and lightened her mood.

Reily, always late, came to the door at six. He sported a white dress shirt and navy blazer. *Not too shabby.* Even his hair looked dapper, proper. She locked the house behind her without a send-off. Work trapped her mother. The same mother who had said, "I'll get a picture of you before your expensive date."

Reily's father drove them to the restaurant. Collen saw him wink at Reily when Reily held open the car door for her. Despite some degree of approval, Mr. Watters let his son do the talking—the few words spoken. Reily didn't loosen up until the maître d' seated them in a private booth with cushions softer than she could imagine.

"That sure is a lot of silverware." Reily followed the comment with a nervous sip from his water glass. A flickering candle at the far end of the table caused the glass to sparkle. Her companion shined too, in his own clumsy, stylish way.

She smoothed her dress. "Thanks for bringing me here. I feel like I'm in a movie."

A waiter in a black blazer and pleated trousers devoid of lint or stain politely requested drink orders. Cokes came back in ten-ounce bottles, baring paper straws swirled pink and white.

They siphoned a portion of the liquid contents, before the fashionable man returned with thin, oblong books. The leather-bound menus were as extravagant as the entrées: chicken cordon bleu, halibut stuffed with crabmeat, filet mignon with a wild mushroom glaze. "What's chateaubriand?" She remembered *chateau* meant house in French.

"I have no idea, and what's béarnaise sauce?" Reily gave a slight smile. "Do you think it's made from bears?" He feigned concern.

Colleen went along, making her eyes gape. "And mayonnaise. It's delicious."

They laughed. Nerves slackened.

For the special feast, she ordered chicken marsala. Reily chose lobster tail with drawn butter. She wondered what "drawn" meant. The foreign jargon, the bedazzling atmosphere . . . she had become Queen Colleen for the night.

The food's arrival put a temporary cork in their conversation. The magnificent meal exceeded expectations by every measure of flavor and appearance. Reily cracked a claw, splattering crustacean juice on his sleeve. She wetted a napkin and scrubbed gingerly. "I have something to tell you." The chore gave an excuse not to witness his reaction.

"Oh?" The utterance contained dread, yet resignation.

"I'm sorry for being distant the past month or so." She let her hand slide down to his and picked up her head. "You know something big has been bothering me, don't you?"

Reily returned her gaze, and nodded.

"What's *your* theory?"

"That's easy. You're moving, aren't you?" He sat back as if waiting for the wallop of his worst fears.

"Wrong." She nibbled on her thumbnail, a subliminal stall before the drop. "I'm changing schools."

Reily did not flinch. "To Bishop Mallory?"

"How did you guess?"

He shrugged, hair obstructing his eyes but not the disappointment. "There aren't many other options, I suppose."

She evaluated him. *He seems a little relieved.* "It could be worse. I thought we were moving to Ohio. Still, I hope it won't be weird, you know . . . new building, new classmates."

"You'll be fine, but why now?"

Colleen extended her lower lip and exhaled. "You haven't seen my grades. Mom threatened this for years, but I figured it would never happen. She can't afford the tuition."

Reily forked a morsel of lobster. "I'll help you study, your grades will rise, and before you know it," he paused to swallow, "you'll be back at W.B. for your junior year."

Such an optimist. "We'll see." She twirled the linguine. "I'll miss seeing you at school."

"Don't worry, you'll still see plenty of me . . . if you'd like."

Colleen chewed, delighting in the earthy-sweet flavor of her selection. "Yes, I'd like that." She gave Reily an appreciative gawk. "You really know how to treat a girl."

A dessert tray made them starry-eyed. Colleen went for chocolate mousse. New York cheesecake won Reily's favor. The cocoa scent, the velvety, over-the-top taste . . . for the first time in her life, she felt like a grownup, an adult out on the town. Never had she known such indulgence—nor such outstanding company.

Behind the Watters's house, yellow flames climbed the split-oak teepee constructed for the occasion, the architecture operating as designed. Superheated logs snarled in protest, but Reily only heard kind words approving of his preparations. Colleen, now wearing outdoor garb, slathered gratitude like icing on the night.

Beside the fire circle, a cooler chilled soft drinks. An extension cord powered an eight-track player. Colleen shined the flashlight while Reily connected the speakers, perspiring with hurry.

"I have something for you." Her words were soft, pleasing.

Reily finished and stood. "I wondered about that mystery package in the car."

"I'll be right back." Colleen scampered to the door of the shed, retrieving the enigmatic thing beside her bag. She returned, out of breath, holding out the gift.

He understood how horses felt, waiting for sugar cubes from a loving hand. His face ached from restraint. Months of confusion and angst went away in one big smile. The swimsuit beauty in the once a year special edition of *Sports Illustrated* failed to compare to the heavenly spectacle called Colleen. Simultaneously devilish and beatific, she personified a shifting, yet captivating flame. "Should we sit by the fire?"

"That would be nice."

On a blanket they sat, pasted side-by-side. Reily peeled away the wrapping in two tears, exposing a varnished hiking stick—stiff, smooth, and slender. He sensed Colleen gauging his reaction.

"I figured you needed an official one with all the hiking you do."

He eyeballed the tight grain with hues the color of honey. "Thanks, it's really cool. I wonder what kind of wood this is."

"I knew you'd ask that." Firelight illuminated Colleen, the angel of Bethlehem. "My brother took me to a store in Stroudsburg. I thought I would get you fishing stuff, but I saw the stick. Anyway, the owner said it's white oak. Supposed to be strong and tough to break."

Reily pretended to bend it, but an urgent cacophony broke the reverie of cellulose. From the front side of the house, Marlin bawled sounds of greeting. Boom and Cindy came past the garden patch with their four-legged escort, followed by Wil and Kelly, the two-timing troublemaker. Wil last mentioned bringing someone, but Reily envisioned alternative, more prudent, prospects. Kelly stood glued to Wil, as if afraid of the surroundings. Perhaps she knew she had dug a deeper hole for the both of them.

Without a "hi" or "hello," Kelly handed Reily a paper bag. "Here," the dangerous one spoke. "Wil said you needed these."

Reily detected clues of attempted kindness. A bounce in her delivery. Upward flexes of cheeks and eyes. "Thanks." He viewed the bag's contents—the three ingredients for s'mores. "We'll make these in a little while." He found Kelly to be more personable than assumed. Shorter and more attractive, too. Still, Colleen had her by a mile.

Reily placed the goods beside a log. "Mr. Wil, help me find roasting sticks."

Wil whispered something to Kelly and came to his aid. "Always making me do stuff . . ."

"Anything to keep you out of trouble."

A wide and weepy silver maple, the bane of his father for its untidy lifestyle, redeemed itself by supplying all the skinny, pliable sticks they could need. Reily sliced them off with a pocketknife from his scouting days.

Wil cradled a bundle. "Thanks for having this soiree, Watters. It's going to be top-notch."

Upon their return to the fire, a most awkward couple sauntered into view. The odd spectacle of Eddie with Rachel jettisoned any lingering doubts. Reily would have to socialize with his *sister*, but so be it. Tonight promised new beginnings—an outstanding, momentary flash in the strange and glorious continuum of time.

Eddie bellowed the bonfire as only Eddie could, with gorilla lungs and bullish determination. Flames reached higher, pulsing heat and light. Boom and Cindy nestled like cooing doves. Wil proffered weird baby talk at Kelly, who numbed herself on alcoholic swill supplied by Eddie. Rachel appointed herself activities director by asking everyone to write down a wish to incinerate at midnight. She distributed pencils and pieces of paper—the premise being to liberate dreams and increase their chances of coming true. Reily considered priority desires. Colleen wrapped an arm around his waist, as if he required a reminder.

The night moved like an endless river, flavored with smoke, sticky chocolate, and tiny sips of Knisely whisky. When the special hour approached, astute Cindy provided the countdown from a bejeweled watch. The hospitality of fire and energy of friends made Reily buoyant. A sweet smacker from Colleen kept him tethered as he tossed in wishes, not one but three: about a creek, a girl, and aptitudes yet discovered.

With the advent of the New Year, the "Spirit of '76" took on new-fangled meaning—adolescent liberation and soul-filling aspirations in his noble little corner of America.

34

Wil gathered with the rest of the Presbyterian youth group in a circle of chairs too small for teenage bodies. Instead of a campfire, this assembly had, at its center, an idealistic reverend with his own brand of fiery fervor.

From prepping Kelly for a physics exam, Wil recalled that eccentricity defined ellipses. This ellipse contained a bevy of eccentrics, from the ever-contemplative Watters to intriguing, inscrutable Colleen. Even Eddie infiltrated the party. Wil feared wrath and pestilence might follow.

He, of course, could be crowned king of the peculiar, verified by self-imprisonment for an hour and a half amongst this brood. But genius is stealth, subtle. Busty, home-schooled twins never missed a youth group meeting. And there was the cleric's daughter. The hyper-blonde object of svelte, sinful yearnings attended Muhlenberg College and lived at home, liberated to assist young Catholic converts in the ways of the faith. Wil welcomed her therapy.

Youth group became a winter, communal exercise. When cold outside, why not find warmth amongst the brethren? His skeptical heart could use the heating. Preached precepts were intellectual fodder, filtered for philosophical and literary nuggets. A writer required infusions of words and ideas to remain nimble.

The pastor orbited, distributing paper cups, followed by his daughter-goddess filling each with spring water. She dribbled drops on Wil's hand, and winced. "Sorry about that."

Wil flicked off the beads. "It's okay." Her killer, covalent eyes reminded him of a James Bond movie temptress.

Say of the Day: providence.

Despite the heaven-sent distraction, he absorbed instructions to pair off, and teamed up with Watters to discuss, of all possible topics, water.

"In Christianity, and other religions, water has much meaning. God uses it as a symbol for salvation, peace, and restoration." The pastor, hip in an olive turtleneck, roamed as he orated. "Take a drink from your cup and think about how it makes you feel."

Wil shrugged. Reily shrugged back. They hydrated in unison.

"So, tell me your thoughts . . . anyone?" The pastor held a goblet, presumably filled with water, unless Eddie spiked it.

"Refreshing," peeped one of the buxom twins.

"Cool," said an unknown boy with a mask of acne.

"Revitalizing," stated Colleen. She found her voice. Reily nudged her in a form of accolade.

Wil wanted the last word. "Tonic."

The pastor grinned. "Excellent reflections. Now, I will give each person a verse to look up. Get a Bible and take a few minutes to find and read your passage, then discuss it with a partner. Think about what it means to you."

Wil plucked a King James from the bookshelf and summoned Reily to a corner, safe from the distraction known as Colleen, but imperiled by the synthetic stench of the church's new carpet. Eddie levitated to the far side of the room, escorted by the preacher's progeny. "How comes Knisley has all the luck?"

Reily sat on the stinky carpet, back against floor-level cabinets. "Eddie's secretly wallowing in misery, but she'll lessen the pain. Every inch of her is perfect. I give him credit though—he'll do anything to 'better' himself for Rachel."

"What's your good word?" Wil wetted his fingers, probing the pages for Isaiah 58.

Reily cleared his throat. "Revelations 22. Here it is, *Then the angel showed me the river of the water of life, as clear as crystal, flowing from the throne of God and of the Lamb.*"

"Makes me hunger for trout with lemon butter . . . and leg of lamb."

Reily regarded him with his head cocked, judging a murderous pagan.

"I can't help it . . . I'm hungry."

"Hold your appetite, there's more to eat. *On each side of the river stood the tree of life, bearing twelve crops of fruit, yielding its fruit every month. And the leaves of the tree are for the healing of the nations.*"

"The old tree of life thing. I heard of that. Is that the place where you learn about reproduction from magazines with centerfolds?"

Reily chuckled, but cringed. "You'll have us turned into salt. Redeem yourself. Recite your assignment."

Wil held the Bible high to block his own face, fearing spasms of inappropriate laughter as he read. "*The LORD will guide you always; he will satisfy your needs in a sun-scorched land and will strengthen your frame*—even your notable superstructure, Watters. Have you been working out or something?" Reily looked sturdier than normal.

"You're hilarious, but observant." Reily flexed his biceps. "I started lifting again."

"*You will be like a well-watered garden, like a spring whose waters never fail.*" Wil closed the book, punctuating the end of his abbreviated sermon.

Reily fiddled with the cuff button on his flannel sleeve. Stringy locks hung from a despondent head. "The spring might hold out, but my swimming's failing. That's for sure."

"At least you're in the game. I'm mad at myself for sitting out this year." Wil meant it. No part of him liked foregoing competition.

"But you're cleaning up on the court. The only cleaning I'm doing is the chicken coop, and Marlin's turds."

"Don't start that lame, feeling sorry for your—"

The pastor interrupted, requesting convergence. He sought volunteers to share the sampled scriptures. When none emerged, he ordained Eddie.

The brawny chosen one might have preferred spontaneous combustion, but the Almighty tagged him this day. He lifted his book to read. "*On the last and greatest day of the festival, Jesus stood and said in a loud voice, 'Let anyone who is thirsty come to me and drink.'*"

Tremors of awkward, uncontrolled giddiness overcame Wil, overflowed to Reily, and set off a chain reaction amongst those who knew Eddie and those that did not. The pastor extinguished the outburst, but with supernatural flare the Holy Spirit had spoken—exposing Eddie's proclivity for potent *illicit* spirits.

35

The Kabumbas' window thermometer hovered at fifty degrees. Outside, pockets of dirty snow melted into mini, muddy wallows. A bird on the ledge peered at Boom, rediscovering its voice and a reason for singing. The February warmth justified a tribute. With daylight rebounding and pavement revealed, running would be a fine form of reverence.

Boom's feet beat the street westward, pulling him forward, faster, past houses in need of a spring cleaning and barking dogs upset over a fallen twig. At the bridge over Mannequin Creek, he opened his gait and chased the sun. Onward for another mile he bounded like an impala before hooking left and winding through a community of mobile homes. A heavyset woman waved, a man in a pickup truck glared. Boom couldn't have cared less—flying made him fearless. At maximum velocity, he merged with the main road and, before crossing the familiar water, exited to the trail ever sublime. While many weeks had lapsed since their last meeting, the Water Way, as he had coined the path that paralleled the creek, invited him back like an old friend.

Muck spattered as he moved along. Boom slowed his pace to see and sense the scenery awakened, kindled back to life for mere hours. Through the drab poked chromatic swabs of green—mosses, bushes, and woody beings cloaked in everlasting plumes. His mind wrote and recorded, piloted by self-steering legs.

The woods exhaled a glad, fusty breath. Stationary, deciduous occupants became disciplined soldiers, ready to defend. One stood out among the rest, a giant on the other side of the creek a hundred feet away, arms aglow and outstretched, pushing away other trees. Boom named it the "stand back" tree.

Cindy infused his rejuvenated mind. That morning, she'd told him of a letter received from Swarthmore—admittance to the Honors College in Biology. She had crushed his hand with excitement. Cindy devoured knowledge like an anteater slurping ants—ideas and facts vacuumed with delight. He worried about their future together. *What will happen when she goes away?* Her parents, pleasant when he met them last month, probably disapproved of their relationship. The apprehension made his sides cramp.

Boom cleared his mind and hastened his pace. The trail became chaotic and indifferent, but the creek consoled without discourse. Serenity held sway on the Water Way.

He reached the far end of the trail at the top of the watershed and rested. Damp from exertion, his body shivered as earth's scant heat ventured to space. In the withered winter backdrop, Boom noticed an interruption of the tree line in the distance—an opening in the unbridled forest. He scrambled to the spot.

Subtle hummocks of fragmented rock mingled with tall tufts of dry grass. Tough, stunted saplings rose along the perimeter. The shadow of the quarry pit lay a stone's throw away. The hardscrabble landscape contrasted with the uniformity around it—a raft adrift on a wooded sea.

The unusual place merited additional examination in better illumination on a different day, with a certain smart, and most studious, girl.

36

Merle monkeyed with the loose side mirror of the Wagoneer, driving the four-wheeled beast to reinforce mastery over his domains, acquired or perceived. Lead partner status afforded minimal perks and a disproportionate hurt from the headaches. While the others schemed and dreamed, he did the lion's share of the work, tracking every aspect of a project like elusive game, until the prize succumbed . . . unless *uncivil* servants gained the upper hand. Not this time.

He parked along the neglected service road, extracted himself from the vehicle, and slammed the door. The mirror fix held—a small harbinger of success. With map in hand, he delved into the dreary forest, a miry mess soon to be the shiny jewel of Eastern Power's expanding energy empire. *Someday.*

Clothed in a wool dress coat, Merle ambled with attentiveness, envisaging hibernation patterns of black bears and venom-laden snakes in a period of unseasonable warmth. Dillon & Reynolds Consulting had ushered unwelcome heat earlier in the month with their discovery of Lenape artifacts on water authority grounds. Such finds were common, but never gratifying, and necessitated additional grid samples and spot digs. Locations for further excavations were at the discretion of the archeological experts, like those employed by the consultant. The *D* and *R* of Dillon & Reynolds had second meaning to preferred customers like Eastern Power: *Discreet* and *Resolute*—resolved to achieve rosy outcomes for each and every well-paying client.

Allies also required quality control, which was the purpose of today's operation. Merle sought to inspect three sites in the northern section—an area destined for inundation. Skinny hardwoods gave him the perspective of a louse in an upside-down hairbrush. He had not lifted a brush or barely a comb since college, but an old girlfriend *had* called him a louse. Indigenous rabble-rousers were bound to resurrect her sentiments when he flooded ancestral lands and drowned every stump. Acknowledgment might assuage their concerns. *Lake Lenape* had appeasing alliteration.

A far, earthen pile matched an X on the map, indicating a required dig. Upon inspection, the squared edges and prodigious volume of the pit caused consternation. Such effort foretold a hefty invoice. The water-filled bottom mocked him. *All this to sort out a few implements and bones.* He exhaled through constrained nostrils, souring on the lake-naming idea.

Merle rotated, setting internal bearings for site number two. In reorienting his inner compass, he traveled arm's length in reverse upon an unstable, overhanging section of pit wall. A pit fall resulted, landing him legs first in the sloppy innards of a D&R mega-depression. Conferring an unexpected angle for examining the progress, he verified that each sheer cut did, indeed, reach the minimum required depth of eight feet. Profanity ensued.

After an epoch of record-high anxiety, Merle emerged from the contracted ravine, covered in chilled clay . . . and desperate for the nearest kiln.

37

Extend. Rest. Extend again. Each of Reily's strained repetitions brought him closer to the vague goal of optimal fitness. Overhead, paddles stirred a conflicting cadence, exacerbating claustrophobia caused by exercising in a dim and damp basement. The ceiling fan labored to turn and failed to move the air. It, too, lacked skill and purpose.

From the barbell dungeon, Reily ascended spent, worn, and worthless. Into the living room he spilled, searching television for Sunday afternoon diversion. Dishwashing negligence grounded Colleen. A basketball tournament in Reading preoccupied Wil. Boom reserved the day to study with Cindy—the productivity of such interludes questionable. Eddie had to organize his dad's basement workshop—every nut, bolt, and screw—instead of touring halls of art at the State Museum in Harrisburg with Rachel and Mom.

Reily languished uninspired on the sofa beside Marlin, pretending to be a pillow. *Deliverance* filled the screen, and the vacuum of his self-worth conundrum. Banjo music and bumpkins lolled him to semi-consciousness.

Whitewater scenes yanked him awake. Hollers over foam and spray. Paddling and action. Potential peril at every turn. Memories of the day on the Lehigh came trickling back—Steve Patterson and his canoe. Canoeing a river made plying a lake a fool's errand. Rivers required skill and interpretation. Canoes were ancient and civilized with sleek symmetry and curvaceous lines. A revelatory jolt spread outward from Reily's core to his extremities. A new calling. Stowed somewhere in the crumby recess of a backpack pocket, lay a business card bearing the number of the paddling man. *Would he remember his invitation?*

After the morose movie ending, internal clouds diverged as afternoon departed. Reily saw himself buffeting waves and gliding like an otter down dogged, phantasmal waterways. He leaped from the cushions and paced the floor. Marlin startled and stared.

Watters the river man—speedy Huck Finn of a new era. Life was reshuffling. The cards fell into place. Swimming became the logical precursor to his pending, waterborne second wind. A paddler must swim, and swim well. Frittering away years along the creek implanted an affection for anything aqueous. Besides Mr. Patterson, Reily knew no serious canoeists. The void provided advantage—a chance to be the one and only, a traveler of a road less traveled.

The empty house ignored his longings. What did it know about self-determination? Marlin understood. He slipped from the sofa, shook off lethargy, and led Reily to the door—a portal to self-discovery.

38

"It's a beautiful piece. We need to get this in a show."

Eddie blushed with pride at Mrs. Watters's comments. A rush of confidence washed over him. Unfamiliar territory. Pop tore him down, this woman sent him to the moon.

Mrs. Watters went to check on Mr. Watters, who had suffered a "setback" and rested in his bedroom. Alone in the studio, Eddie repacked the instruments of his craft like precious jewelry in a case. Two basketball shoes tromped into view, attached to a sturdy, not so well-groomed friend.

"You look more like Reily every day. Do you two wear the same wigs?"

Wil pretended to kick him. "Wow, you're a painter *and* a comic? Such talent."

Eddie snapped the box of watercolors and brushes shut. "Jethro, what do you think of that?" He pointed to an easel supporting a masterful work—a mill along a golden stream with a willow draping its shore.

Wil stepped closer for examination. "Reily's mom sure can paint."

"That's mine."

"She *gave* it to you?" Wil's words dripped with jealousy.

Eddie stood by his side. "No, *I* painted it."

Wil said nothing, and restudied the watery scene at close range. "This is incredible. Good going, Knisley. I mean it."

The praise carried extra weight. Wisecracks were Wil's trademark. Reily normally dished out the compliments. "Thanks. I'll give you one of my paintings someday."

"Preferably one with naked ladies."

"We'll need to find models." Eddie appraised Wil. "Where'd you come from?" The Watters's house could double as a hotel. One never knew who might drop in.

"Reily's room. He's a lump back there, engrossed in a book about canoeing. I think Marlin's reading it, too."

"He's bummed out about the last meet." Eddie dropped his volume. "His mom said he missed making districts."

Wil nodded. "But I don't think he cares that much. He's worried about his dad."

"Hey, I heard Kelly and Troy broke up. What gives?"

"We'll see." Wil made a skeptical snarl. "I don't know if it will last. She's flakey."

"He tried to give me flack today on the way to the bus."

"Who? Troy?"

"Yep. He said, 'You and your gay friends are dead meat.'" Eddie did his best imitation of Troy's whiney voice and oafish demeanor. Troxell might have been built like a badger, but he knew better than to test Eddie. He had Troy by inches and pounds, and the bonus of a sadistic reputation.

"What did you say?"

"Bite my weenie, Troxell."

Wil smiled—the devious sort. "Perfect."

"He's a punk, that's all, but I'd watch it. He's still mad at you for stealing his girly."

Wil shrugged it off. "Where's Rachel?"

"Back in her room, I guess." The art lesson had consumed all his thoughts—distracting from her rousing magnetism—as had the ride to the house, seeing the Kemp property become a heavy equipment parking lot. "Did you see the bullshit next door?" Eddie cast his head the direction of the neighboring former farm.

"Makes me sick. I'm writing a letter to the editor about it."

"Nobody thinks about animals and *their* homes, that's the damn problem. People would rather have Kmarts and shopping malls." Eddie felt a surprising degree of frustration. Aloofness made for an easier life.

"Kmart does have a slick selection of fishing gear . . ." Wil had that faraway look. "Trout season's coming up. My last free year of angling. Next spring, I'll have to pay for a stupid license."

"Welcome to Club Sixteen, reserved for adults-in-training."

Wil shook his head in disgust. "Let's go bug Reily. He's next to join the club."

39

Boom led Cindy on a private adventure . . . a return to the lavish lands of the Mannequin watershed. Spring had almost sprung, the vernal equinox only a week away. Swollen buds and restless birds exhibited clues to a forthcoming transformation—incited by an annual journey around the closest star. In yesterday's class, Mr. Kreider reaffirmed the positioning and importance of the earth and sun relationship in his dry, witted way. With direct rays upon the equator, daylight and darkness would soon be equal for a day.

In the universe, nothing is static. Movement is constant. The daily shine lengthens until the summer solstice, and then begins a slow motion retreat as the planet keeps moving on. Boom found it all to be miraculous.

This year's precision revolution had proven quite a trip thus far. Good experiences, abundant and delighting, overwhelmed the bad moments, mostly brief and forgettable. With running as a mode of travel, he had mastered his local world. With Cindy, he had captured a kindred spirit to partake in his conquests . . . benign as they may be.

Cindy, under the visible influence of cosmological bliss, talked at the speed of falling water, bouncing from thing to thing. Listening imparted voluminous enjoyment. Words and messages floated on bubbly air all the way to his exuberant heart. Personal rapture. Rhapsody in emergent green.

"I'm so glad to be hiking, Boom." She paused beside a large rock wearing a mottled beard of lichen. In the vibrant light, the pale savannah hues matched Cindy's eyes. "It makes me feel good."

"Yes, me too." Such an emotion exceeded articulation.

This dreamland belonged to them alone. In town, parents washed cars and tinkered with lawnmowers while kids tried on leather mitts, prepping for baseball tryouts. Seeing Luckenbach Falls in its prime made the other pursuits seem trivial by comparison.

An outsized tree on the steep valley wall wore a diagonal slash of orange paint on its trunk. Boom adjusted his vision, scanning beyond. Other hefty forest specimens shared the mark. He made sure Cindy saw them, too.

"They're going to cut them, aren't they?" He'd never heard her voice so sad.

"I presume they are." Boom acquired regal language and pronunciation from his father and mimicked it without forethought, but "presume" seemed appropriate when speaking of impending death and ruination to organisms he thought of as introverted friends. "We should keep going. I want to show you what I found."

Moments passed without conversation. Cindy broke the lull. "When does track begin?"

"We've already had two practices. I forgot to tell you." Boom moderated his response—usually he gave her too much information in heavy daily doses.

"And which events? Please don't say pole vault." Cindy flashed perfect teeth, neat and orderly like her personality.

"I'm trying the longer races—the eight-eighty, one mile, and, I think, the two mile."

"That sounds exhausting."

Boom guffawed. "No, I can do it. I know I can." His training routine had expanded, along with the distances covered. Confidence had reached new heights.

"I bet you can, too." She grasped his hand as if to prove it.

"There's only one other person who runs the two mile at our school."

"Who?"

"A boy named Troy. The one who has difficulty controlling his anger."

"Oh no."

"Oh yes." Boom envisioned, but did not fear, an unavoidable showdown.

"You're going to humble him, you watch." Cindy's words could uplift mountains.

"He holds the record at the school."

"Don't you mean, *held* it?"

Boom restrained a smile. "We will see." A squirrel clowned and cowered. Crows chortled unintelligible gossip. *Maybe the birds were speaking about them . . . the unlikely couple.*

"We need to go that way." Boom motioned to his right. His left hand remained in hers. "It isn't much further."

The forest yielded to the ratty patch he remembered, the periphery tasseled with clumps of grass and thwarted trees. A small area contained a cluster of cattails with wiry stalks rooted in stagnant water.

Cindy treaded one step at a time across the open space—an otherworldly astronaut on a moonwalk. "It's really unique. Check out all the rocks."

Rocks there were. Piles galore. "They must be from the quarry."

Cindy put a finger on her lips, waved him over, and kneeled. In front of her, merely a yard away, a foot-long snake lay in a stupor. The color of chlorophyll, it posed in stark contrast to the gray slate beneath. In bright sunlight, the dark substrate served as a warming bed, coaxing the animal to awaken.

Her eyes locked on the harmless reptile. "I'm seeing Mr. Kreider's poster. I think it's a green snake."

"Yes, you might be right." Boom positioned himself on hands and knees. "If I remember, there are two kinds, smooth and rough. I don't know the difference."

Cindy raised her fair, fine brows. "I don't know either, but I'm memorizing every detail."

They left the snake to bask and searched for other finds. Boom uncovered rusty bolts. Cindy discovered a relic beer bottle of a discontinued brand. Treasure hunting occupied another easygoing hour. Boom felt older and bolder when they were together, a greater awareness about his direction in life. Like a trusted compass, Cindy showed him true bearings. He would follow them, and her, wherever they led.

40

Merle read a courtesy letter from Harrisburg regulators as he leaned over a chef salad at a Newark eatery. Across the table, his business partner crunched a crouton from a competing Caesar.

Merle reread the date mentioned in the document and shuddered. April 30th. Major hurdle number two—the promised day for a decision by the Pennsylvania Department of Environmental Resources, and fifteen days before a prospective ruling of the Federal Power Commission. A negative Commission edict would terminate the project. He rated their prospects at ninety percent . . . favorable odds for a non-betting man.

His late father gambled all the time. Real estate played proxy for slots and ponies. An acquisition here, a rental property there. Ballooning mortgage payments. Rising city taxes. Too much stress. One too many bottles of booze. Dad's dithering life abruptly terminated by an ill-placed telephone pole on an unforgiving curve.

The life insurance check paid for the last years of college, and Merle vowed never to make the same mistakes. Prudence and sobriety imbued decisions. If the latest endeavor ended due to unforeseen circumstances, Merle had other ventures planned, permitted, and operating. The most lucrative had proven to be a medical waste incinerator on the poor side of Richmond. Eastern Power purchased cogenerated electricity and resold it at a guaranteed profit. The planned Mannequin project meant steady green without the guilt of toxic emissions, or, God forbid, an unrecoverable loss of millions.

"Don't worry. Everything seems tight," the chubby partner said, spitting a few drops of creamy dressing. "The bank is pleased."

"For now." The morning meeting had gone well. The financiers, hoodwinked by hydro, dismissed the well-known, decades-long Tocks Island Dam controversy, blaming the Delaware River project's failure on its sheer grandiosity. Merle sipped a cooling cup of coffee. "This is the waiting game I hate."

A framed poster on the interior brick wall commemorated the first Earth Day, as if it were mocking him. The waitress, likely complicit in the art selection, scurried around in a florid dress, smiling to ingratiate herself. Whatever warped politics she embodied, her looks were divine. He self-consciously tightened his abdomen and leveled unruly, thread-bare tufts upon his crown.

The partner sensed the maneuver and glanced at the scurrying enchantress. "Don't get your hopes up, Merle. She is ten years too young, and probably eats Grape Nuts. You know the type."

Merle did, or so he assumed. That was all he ever made . . . assumptions. Sometimes they left him lonely—or, even worse, wealth deprived.

41

School lunch lacked pizazz without a Colleen meetup. Months after her banishment to Bishop Mallory High, Reily still missed the tender midday commiserations over pizza and shakes.

The occasion of his birthday made her absence more acute, although two girls in his grade slipped him happy wishes on folded notes during English. The teacher would surely disapprove of their misuse of contractions.

That morning, the newspaper delivered his horoscope, promising a year of accomplishments and new adventures. For the first time, he learned that Herb Alpert and Cesar Chavez shared his March 31st birthday. The tune of "This Guy's in Love with You" occasionally floated off Mom's lips, entranced while she painted. Dad referred to Chavez as a bit of a rabble-rouser. To Reily, based on TV news, the man simply stood up for the rights of people living desperate lives.

Eddie carried an overladen tray like an immense toddler lost in a Bonanza Steakhouse. He sat down and shimmied closer. "What's up, Jethro? Are you contagious or something?"

"Very funny." Encased in his own deliberations, Reily failed to realize the empty perimeter around him. "Nice to see you, too."

"When are you getting your license?"

"That's right, I'm sixteen." Reily faked amazement.

Eddie unwrapped the school's rendition of a Big Mac. "When you start driving, the chicks will be all over you."

"I'm in no hurry to drive, plus it doesn't work that way."

"What? Are you insane? I want to go for the exam again."

"You'll pass, don't worry—everybody does their third try." Reily speared a few tater tots. "I have this feeling that once I begin motoring, I'll stop riding my bike."

Eddie stared as if striving to comprehend advanced algebra. "So?"

The flannel lines on Reily's sleeve became roads leading through the neighborhood. "We'll forget what fun it is . . . and spend time further away."

Eddie's leer remained fixed. "You're losing me."

"Nothing will be the same."

Eddie shrugged with an exaggerated grimace. "Nah, it's all groovy."

Reily wanted that to be true. Despite his coarse character, Eddie had a subtle way of smoothing things out. You couldn't stay down with the big guy around.

That evening before dinner, Reily placed his hands on the contoured wheel of Leviathan, with his father secured in the front passenger seat— the natural position for a copilot. Wil had named the Chevy sedan for a reference in *20,000 Leagues Under the Sea*. Reily hoped for a maiden voyage devoid of squid, skids, and over-the-road peril.

"Do you have your learner's permit with you?" Keith Watters asked, thorough as always, voice steady and calm, although he had yet to regain his pre-heart attack weight and color.

Reily rechecked his coat pocket. "Yep, right here."

"Watch carefully at the end of the driveway. Head toward Mowery Road."

"Where are we going?"

"A long route to town. I want you to log a few miles, and make a stop at Bergman's Hardware. I need to pick up a new chain for the saw, and if you and your friends are going to have more campfires, I want to see if I can order one of those metal rings—like you see at park campsites."

"That'd be really cool."

Dad nodded his head. "I thought you'd think so."

The world whooshed by. Speed exhilarated. The car lurched whenever Reily stepped on the gas. Stopping brought minor whiplash. Eight cylinders and power brakes proved an ungainly combination, requiring experience to master, but the outing exceeded prior assumptions.

The test came downtown: pedestrians, stoplights, stop signs, and, the ultimate quandary, parallel parking. After four attempts, his father left the car without explanation, and commenced directing traffic. Reily managed to position Leviathan a foot from the curb.

Inside Bergman's, he beelined to the modest sporting goods inventory while his father scavenged the tools aisle. A man stooped to read the fine print on a box for a bicycle tire inner tube. The guy appeared outdoorsy and familiar. When he returned upright, Reily recognized him as Canoe Steve.

"Mr. Patterson?"

The man reviewed him, perplexed. "Wait a minute . . . we met on the river a while back, but I forget your name. See what happens when you get older."

"It's Reily. Reily Watters."

"Oh yeah. Sorry. That's a great name. I should have remembered." Mr. Patterson returned the box to the shelf. His forearms were the size of fence posts. "What brings you to the hardware store?"

"I'm with my dad. I drove. I'm working on getting my license."

"Boy, I remember getting mine. I think my father aged ten years teaching me to drive."

Reily smiled a little. He liked Steve Patterson's lighthearted manner. "I'm glad I ran into you. I wanted to give you a call."

"Uh-oh, what did I do?"

"You offered to take me canoeing. I enjoyed paddling on the Lehigh and wondered if you wouldn't mind getting me out on the water again?"

"Hmmm." Steve stroked his own chin as if chewing on the idea, then grinned wider than the store. "Heck yes. Anytime. I wish I could take everyone canoeing. What are you doing this Saturday?"

"I'm not sure. I don't think anything in particular."

"I planned to run a section of the Schuylkill River near Hawk Mountain. You can be my bowman."

Reily saw churning rapids and forest-clad canyons. He tasted adrenaline. "I'll check with my dad."

"You'll do what?" Keith Watters spoke behind him, in jest.

Before Reily could make introductions, gregarious Steve saved him the effort. With permission quickly granted, Dad and the canoe man were comparing notes on eastern rivers. Dad relayed observations gleaned from the sky, and Steve confirmed or corrected, based on his own ground level, cruising reconnaissance.

Arrangements were set for Saturday. Roads became rivers on the drive home.

At the house, Reily's mother greeted her son in the kitchen. "How did it go?" Her excessive enthusiasm flagged a secret. After sixteen years of interaction, he read her like a neon sign.

Reily slipped off his coat. "Okay, I think." His father nodded at his mother. Nothing else said. Approval Keith Watters style.

"A pretty young lady stopped by while you two were gone."

Reily perked. "What?"

"Her name is Colleen, I believe." Karen Watters winked. "And she gave you this." Fancy wrapping enclosed a semi-rigid, rectangular item, flawlessly swathed and taped.

At the kitchen table, Reily deflected Marlin's prying muzzle and peeled away the paper to expose a softbound book entitled *Big Trees of Pennsylvania*, complete with photos, sketches, and descriptions of the record-sized specimen of every species of tree found in the Keystone State. The champion sycamore exceeded twenty-two feet in circumference. The tallest white pine towered more than one hundred and eighty feet. The pages that most caught his eye spoke of a whale of a white oak in Chester County, alive for over three hundred years and rivaling the sycamore in width. When it had germinated, native people ruled the land and William Penn had yet to sow seeds in the future United States.

The detailed drawing triggered thoughts of another stately white oak surviving along the Mannequin Creek—a gentle, spreading giant awaiting its twentieth-century fate.

42

In the stale light of his bedroom, Wil, casual and comfortable in basketball shorts, pondered mixed feelings prompted by the cessation of a troublesome relationship. Kelly had comprehensively kyboshed her ties to Troy. While the durability of the Troy-Kelly courtship had been dubious to date, Wil had indulged the fruits of her infidelity. Her declaration of new independence posed palpable risks to his longevity. In her final confessions to Troy, Kelly admitted to relations with a certain suave ninth grader, and bragged about the freshman's romantic talents. The countdown of the doomsday clock had commenced.

Hutzpah came naturally to Wil. Self-defense did not. Deep within, he abhorred violence. The one punch ever thrown missed the intended face and struck a fire extinguisher, resulting in bruised knuckles. He would much rather talk his way out of a predicament, but Troy did not seem inclined to cool-headed acquiescence. Wil saw himself in a disturbing new light—*closet wuss.*

He put down *Jane Eyre*, ostentatious required reading unfurling a fateful tale of tribulations and yearnings of a different era. In this moment, Wil yearned for the kind of fulfillment his mom's cookies or cupcakes provided . . . a sugary rush not altogether different from the surge induced by succulent contact with Kelly Bingham. His feelings for the girl had matured, evolved. He went in search of treats.

While masticating at the kitchen counter, Wil gazed in a daze out the window. April harkened outdoor drying season. The sexy woman across the way, in heels and office attire, clipped laundry to a line—shirts, sheets, and *was that a negligee?*

Wil cleansed his throat and mind with a glass of milk, and returned upstairs to a muddled bedroom. The bodacious air-drying neighbor withered in comparison to his dangerous liaison. He saw the first two months of secret interactions with Kelly as the "Physical Stimulation Phase"—light on talk, heavy on body contact. Now, they had entered the "Intellectual Linking Phase," appreciating one another's mind and being, and supplementing fleshly attraction. But the whole adventure had taken a deadly turn. He needed a survival strategy. He needed Reily's counsel.

An unrepentant fly looped his head and the Charlotte Brontë book in his hands, before landing on the wall. Wil abbreviated the insect's pit stop with a swift, backside thwack of a lined tablet. Squished, bloody residue remained. A morbid omen of his own impending fate.

Say of the Day: portentous.

43

Mutations and mutagens failed to excite Boom, although watching Cindy distribute a handout on DNA fingerprinting supplied an agreeable distraction. Today's lesson centered on applied genetics. Mr. Kreider had returned from a two-week hiatus for emergency surgery. He retained a sly, cerebral aura in spite of his gallbladder's removal.

Two rows away, Reily doodled on a notebook, drawing boats of some sort.

"Mr. Watters." Kreider interrupted his own explanation, startling the class. "Are you sketching gene sequences?"

Reily flipped his notebook to the next page and slid lower in his seat. "No, sir."

"We're curious about your subjects. Please, do share."

Reily did not lift his head. "Canoes. They're canoes, but I was paying attention." His quiet voice rose to a pleading whimper. Boom never saw him so embarrassed.

Classmates giggled. Mr. Kreider let his admonishing glare linger. "I hope so." Kreider resumed "mutant" talk of physical and chemical causes.

Boom opened his eyes wider to be sure to stay awake.

At the conclusion of class, he and Cindy approached the teacher, now seated with his feet upon the desk. "Mr. Kreider, Cindy and I want to ask you another snake question."

Kreider looked at both of them, holding in his amusement. Boom guessed he found them to be funny, science nerds of two different shades. "Alright," he said, and folded his arms.

Cindy took the lead. "A couple of weeks ago, we were hiking near the headwaters of the Mannequin Creek and found what we think might have been a rough green snake." She looked toward the Pennsylvania snake poster, as if to verify.

Mr. Kreider slid his chair toward a short, two-rowed shelf crammed full of books, and pulled out a thick, hardbound volume on reptiles and amphibians. He swiped through the pages until settling on one in particular. Boom spotted the Latin words *Opheodrys aestivus* at the top. The teacher lowered his glasses, leaned back, and read. "Says here that this species is threatened in Pennsylvania." He lifted his eyes at the two of them. "Are you sure this is what you saw?"

"I think so." Cindy repositioned to see the book. "It had big eyes, just like that one, and a skinny neck." Boom loved her curiousity. She couldn't care less about the social drama of high school and other mundane things.

Mr. Kreider traced his finger along the text. "Was it in a tree?"

"We discovered it on the ground . . . in rocks by a quarry." Boom felt like a scientist, adding to the account of the unique sighting.

"This species is arboreal. It prefers trees." Kreider turned to the next page and scanned for details. "Ah-ha, in contrast, the smooth green snake likes open areas and is much more common." He raised the book and showed them the competition's picture. "They look a whole lot alike. I bet you saw the smooth green snake."

Cindy became a raptor, eyes blazing at the image. "I disagree. I still believe it was the other one." Her skin glowed pink and passionate, framed by a bright and angular hairdo, like an operative in a spy movie.

"Go look for it again. Try and get a picture." Mr. Kreider closed the book and inserted it into its resting place.

Cindy's expression turned desolate. She stared down at Kreider, still in his omnidirectional chair. "It's where the reservoir will go."

"Then tell the authorities you believe there could be a Pennsylvania endangered species on the property and it should be investigated." Despite a temperamental reputation, Kreider had a lot of heart. "And in the meantime, you and Mr. Kabumba can try and ascertain the situation for yourselves. Document the animal. Prove it is there. Also, research the Tellico Dam and the snail darter. It's a big issue. There might be a few lessons you can apply to this situation."

Boom looked at Cindy. Cindy looked at Boom. The recommendations roused him, a pungent awakening, akin to a whiff of formaldehyde from a specimen bottle. Kreider dismissed them, saying he had to go to a staff meeting.

In the hall, they plotted strategy. Cindy doubled down on the idea for a letter to the government. Boom concurred. "But let's get Wil's help."

"He's only in ninth grade."

Boom beamed like a jolly psychic. "Yes, but he writes like Charles Dickens."

44

The morning's adventure had Reily primed. Being with Colleen at her house added high-octane fuel.

"The last part was the best. The river went downhill and the rapids were constant, not big and scary, but fun and wet, not soaking wet, but a splash, then another, and another." He spoke with his hands, dramatizing the motion. "You get the idea."

"Sounds like you had a good time." Colleen gave him half a smile, and half her interest.

Reily tried not to worry. "The Schuylkill is beautiful . . . different from what I expected. One section had this tunnel of rhododendrons. The sun came out, and it looked like a jungle."

"Any tigers?" She got up from the living room sofa. "Do you want a Coke?

"No thanks." The pep from paddling had yet to wear off. When Steve dropped him off at home two hours ago, he gushed compliments. *"No spills, incidents, or complaints. I would have thought you were a seasoned whitewater canoeist."* Steve promised more outings. A trip on the Delaware. Someday, the Susquehanna. Reily hoped so. Mile after mile, the Schuylkill River had thrilled—a continuous, wondrous serpentine of discovery.

Colleen returned with a bottle of soda and flopped down, further away than he wished. In the kitchen, he heard Mrs. Mills, the seldom-seen mom. Colleen scratched at the bottle's logo with her thumbnails.

Someone had to make conversation. "I know I already told you this, but I love the tree book. It's really interesting."

She stared past him. "I'm glad you like it." Her focus returned. "So Wil might get his butt kicked?"

"He's definitely at risk. Troy knows everything."

"Yeah, you mentioned that."

"I have his back, but I told him to be careful."

"Advice from Reily." A guileful nod, hints of old Colleen. Her sly candor and sweet cleverness always kept him guessing what she might do next. Rarely bubbly, she also never seemed angry or sad. The girl had few meanders, but the perfect gradient.

"Whatever it takes." He pulled himself closer. "As soon it gets a little warmer, we're going to camp along the Mannequin. Want to come along?"

Her eyes penetrated his. She had something to say, but wouldn't say it. "Maybe. I don't know if my mom will let me."

She doused his fire. Enthusiasm drained away. "I told Mr. Patterson about the creek, about all the great times along it. He knew about the dam project. He knows a lot about everything. Do you know what the word Mannequin means?"

Colleen resumed studying cursive script on the bottle. "I have no idea . . ."

"Wolf. The Algonquin word is actually 'mahingan,' but white settlers twisted it to Mannequin." He prattled like a grade school geek. "It's neat to think there were once wolves around here, and people who appreciated the bounty of the land."

"Yeah." The detached response increased his discomfort. *Does she have early onset hearing loss?* Her blue eyes lacked sparkle. Cascading brunette tresses had lost their typical luster.

Fatty smells wafted from the kitchen with the sputters and spits of a frying frenzy—the sizzle there making up for the lack of sizzle in the living room.

"Mom's doing burgers, I think."

"Yum." The only thing he could think to say. No dinner offers came. Despite Colleen's chill, Reily's attraction had not waned. He swooped in for a kiss. Their lips squished and bumped in a monotonous mashup of record-short duration, followed by grueling muteness.

"I'm going to use the bathroom. Be right back." Reily fled to the safety of the hallway powder room. Colleen's hairbrush, curling iron, and facial scrub staked claim to the glorified closet, as did a textbook, protected in a homemade book cover lacking word art trumpeting her love for Reily. Tucked in the pages, a bookmark protruded. He followed the tassel and stared. The tag celebrated a uniformed Kyle, #2, cornerback, gridiron stud. The fleshy, beach boy blond Bishop Mallory shrimp held his helmet with insolence.

In heartbreak, Reily wished for a duel, maybe a joust, to secure, for the last time, Colleen's steadfast, unambiguous adoration.

45

Merle patrolled his office, stewing over a letter from the state, delivered days before their communicated decision date. The contents sowed confusion throughout his bodily organs and an imagined cessation of blood flow. *More* studies would be required before *any* permit decision.

Merle had contacts in the environmental department, and one call provided a backstory as painful as a kidney stone. With obvious help from deranged adults, a kid named Wisnoski had written a searing letter about rare and precious snakes on the water authority lands. Snakes, of all things. *Who gives a crap about snakes?* The department wanted a biological survey conducted within thirty days. He would have it to them in ten.

Two days prior, the Federal Power Commission requested a tour of the project grounds—explained by insiders as a pro forma exercise. Merle felt little consolation. Dogwoods bloomed outside the office window, but their velvety, petal-laden grandeur seemed like flowers at a funeral.

If the Commission had omnipotence, maybe they could put a kibosh on the state nonsense. *Fat chance.* Merle's sinuses throbbed, agitated by the lemony odorant of furniture polish. He had ordered the Wednesday cleaning crew to use unscented products. *No one listens anymore.*

Before lunch, he consulted the partners and the Power Commission and coordinated respective calendars. The federal cavalcade would come to town the second Monday in May and receive a red-carpet sampler of Eastern Power's latest clean energy panacea. His secretary had already received a call back from Eco Associates, a new subsidiary of Dillon & Reynolds. The pricey bio sleuths promised to scrub the woods posthaste in search of sensitive species. They assured it would be an "all hands on deck" effort to meet the timeline.

Merle clicked his pen. *Too many hands to feed with my hard-earned cash.*

Compared to Karen Watters's studio, Eddie found painting in his own bedroom akin to scrawling renderings on a cave wall. The lack of light handicapped decisions on the ideal pigments. Rather than inspire, the dimness made him listless. At this pace, the new work would be finished in years, not weeks.

On the bright side, three satisfying things seasoned his day. First, Rachel had made her higher education decision. Dickinson College appeared to be two hours away and a straight shot west. From what he read, it matched her passions and persona. The big city schools, like NYU, made him nervous. Too many distractions. At a little school in Carlisle, he had a better chance of remaining her favorite Ed. After anticipating life as a Red Devil, Rachel had thrown him another bone—the May campout idea sounded good to her. A second small victory. She asked about tents. He said he would "figure it out." If there were a slogan to describe his inner workings, "why worry" would be it.

The third big moment occurred at four o'clock on his way back to the cavern after foraging for a snack in the kitchen. His father, transiting from bathroom to living room, paused at Eddie's bedroom door and pointed. Eddie froze in his tracks. "What?"

"That's not bad."

"Huh?" Unless his ears were malfunctioning, his father had offered a sort of compliment.

"The picture. It's pretty good." Dad's facial expression held a sterile neutrality but, in the old man's way of doing things, the utterance carried profound meaning.

"I'm working on it," Eddie replied. Nothing more needed said.

46

Reily loaded the dishwasher, plate by plate, considering what his friends might be doing on this balmy Saturday night. Olfactory treasures of mowed lawns and mystery blossoms slunk through the opened window. He wondered if Colleen had a date with number two, the pass defender, who probably planned her interception, and egregious "holding," unless she *actually* had the stomach flu.

At the kitchen table, his father unfolded and ogled papers, making audible grunts and sighs during his review.

"I want to show you these." Dad spoke over his glasses, glancing toward him. "These are the drawings for the hydro project." He maintained the gaze, letting the importance sink in. "I got them from the township."

Reily filled the detergent receptacle, started the machine, and dried his hands. Dad oriented the papers on the table for optimal viewing.

"See this." Keith Watters touched a pencil to a skinny pair of lines following a linear feature labeled Mannequin Creek. "It's an access road. It would go up the east side, the whole way to the dam, and on around to the far end of the reservoir."

"Right through the woods where we fish and mess around."

"It gets worse." His father slid the document closer. "These symbols show fishing access points. There is a bunch of these nodes. Guess they figure that more people might come to the creek, and they want to channel them to different spots. I imagine there would be benches and trash cans . . . that sort of thing."

Reily saw voracious anglers crowding the creek bank, and litter along the shores—the secret havens of his childhood paved and made public.

He deliberated over the drawings. The road wormed right past the location of the big oak tree, past beech groves, through mountain laurel jungles, and across the tributary with native brook trout. Due to the slope of the land, it veered before the loch, but continued its ascent. The site of the dam leapt off the paper, a crescent pointing upstream, near the drop of Luckenbach Falls. The falls would fall never again, entombed for the ages in a vault of concrete.

"Dad, why is this allowed? The forest doesn't get a say."

His father folded the documents and creased the edge, as if pressing down for extra punishment. "It isn't right, but it's not over yet. Mr. Wisnoski told me Wil wrote a letter to the state?"

"A really outstanding one."

"See. Maybe that will make a difference. Oh, and I have a tiny bit of favorable news, too." He paused, enduring a momentary, undisclosed, but obvious pain. "Have you noticed what's going on at Kemp's?"

"Not much, from what I've seen."

"Exactly." Dad grabbed his wrist, a gesture reserved for the most serious moments of father to son reinforcement. "Things are at a standstill. There are whispers of bankruptcy. That could be conjecture, but I'm going to poke around."

Marlin interrupted, ambivalent but pleased that his favorite humans were gathered for his entertainment.

"I'm taking Marlin for a long walk." Furry ears stiffened at Reily's declaration.

Marlin led the way to the back door and the leash hanging on a hook.

Mild air fueled their steps as they meandered street to street. On this dreamy night, everything ripened . . . lilacs marked property lines, daffodils aligned in neat rows, spinach awakened in garden plots. Spring peepers whistled from the willows in Swanson's marsh, protected by a barricade of cattails daring to inundate the world with fluffy seeds. Opportunity in all its dimensions blended with bitter reality in the form of invisible earthmovers standing by to erase the realms of childhood.

Behind the marsh spread the complex where Reily and his friends learned their place in the hierarchy of little league baseball. Three years in the outfield taught him the travails of mediocrity. Wil, of course, exceeded—his fastball still recollected with dread. Eddie, slow as a box turtle base to base, achieved simultaneous batting milestones: record-holder for most home runs *and* strikeouts in a C-team season.

On evenings like these, lovers rendezvoused at the ball fields, seeking privacy in and around the dugouts, or so lore had it. Reily never had such a foray, although an interlude with the right girl under the stars, behind the equipment shed, carried zesty appeal. *Was Colleen the right one?*

A freewheeling stonefly struck him in the cheek, a subtle slap to the face and cosmic wake-up call. How could Colleen not feel well? With the big dipper overhead, and Marlin trotting like a wolf on a moose trail, it felt good to be alive, despite assorted predicaments.

The dog caught a new scent passing behind the midget field, and whimpered. Reily heard talking. Heads peeked up behind the backstop.

"Are you spying on us, Marlin?" An unmistakable voice.

"Marlin wants to roam. What are you kids up to?"

"What do you think?" Even in dull light, Wil beamed shamelessly.

"Hi Reily." Kelly spoke, her tone sleepy, but upbeat.

Reily prepared to let one-on-one infield practice resume, but two other players appeared in left field, headed their direction along the foul line.

"Wisnoski," bemoaned a human body with the head of a rat. "You couldn't leave well enough alone."

Reily moved to arbitrate—to prevent two dingbats from clubbing Wil—but a chain-link fence stood in the way. He ran to round the dugout and position himself for intervention. Troy Troxell approached Wil while his long-limbed friend, called "the pickerel" by some, fumed at Reily, waiting for his advance.

Reily raced for home plate. Marlin's leash slipped from his grasp. Everything slowed. Troy lashed out at Wil, inches from his confounded face. A gut punch followed, solid like the sound of a pitch meeting its mark in the center of a mitt. Wil dropped. Kelly screamed at Troy. The two-legged pike swung at Reily's head with a scraggy arm and missed. Fish boy reloaded, misdirecting anger at an innocent dog. A glancing kick. A pained yelp. Reily responded in an out-of-body blur, pouncing first upon the pike, before redirecting fury at Troy. The taunts and injustices of years primed a pent-up walloping lasting a mere forty-five seconds.

Reily breathed hard, standing over Troy—dazed and immobile from the pain of injury and the weight of embarrassment. Marlin snarled like a cougar, jowls at the tender thighs of Pikey, pinned against the dugout. Reily called to his dog, and checked over his shoulder. Wil, baffled, nodded back. Kelly stood by, in suspended animation, the shock of the confrontation—and rebuttal—still raw.

Troy struggled onto his hand and knees. "Get away from me."

"No more." Reily issued the commandment and stepped away. The enemy said nothing. Wil, Kelly, and Marlin joined the walkout.

Once out of earshot, Reily had questions. "What happened back there?"

"Your weight lifting paid off." Wil's wit had already returned.

"I can't remember part of it. I went crazy when they hurt Marlin."

"You dribbled his head."

"Whose head?" Scenes flashed in Reily's foggy mind.

"Troy's—right on home plate. You used it as a pile driver. Your guard dog took care of the kicker. He's a top-notch pup."

Reily gave an appreciative tug on the leash. Marlin respired at a thousand pants per minute. "So, are you okay?"

"Me?" Wil tested his ribs. "A little sore, that's all."

Kelly slipped her arm around Wil's waist. "What do you think Troy will do next?"

"Nothing. Watters humiliated him." Wil regarded Reily. "Thanks for having my back."

Reily strode onward. "Always." He didn't know the hour of the day, where they were going, or the substance of what had transpired. Awash in a great oneness, he sailed overland, powered by the eternal escapades of friendship—strong enough to weather all pandemonium.

47

Wil longed for the messianic presence of the pastor's deified daughter, but she must have had diversionary priorities. The ranks were thin for the church's youth group finale. No Colleen either. She had rejected Reily's invitation, stating uninventively the need to finish a writing assignment—probably her new beau's love letter du jour. Eddie bailed to touch up his painting, possible code for a get-together with Rachel. Wil wondered if he should have invited Kelly for sprightly, wholesome companionship.

On the courtyard turf they lounged, druids reveling in nature. For an icebreaker, the pastor asked them to tell the group about something that gave them great personal joy. A short, pimpled kid mentioned music. "Softball," said one of the busty twins, a torso of consolation in the absence of the revered daughter. Reily hesitated and muttered, "Canoeing."

Wil had three candidates, but one bubbled to the top. "Fishing." What he preferred to be doing at that very moment.

After prayers and meditations, the flock dispersed to find "examples of the beauty and wonder of God's world." Wil believed the twins to be ample evidence, but nonetheless ambled to the edges of the fertilized plot of green in pursuit of creative glory.

An old springhouse sat at the corner of the property, a relic of days past. Never had he inspected the stone structure, nor realized the generous flow seeping from beneath—a skinny, waist-deep run disappearing into a thicket of red-twigged dogwoods. Wil got low and crawled to the edge. Two seven-inch brook trout hovered, inches off the bottom, facing upstream like salmon returning from the sea. They were returning to the risen water. Gifts from the spirit upstairs.

The human Watters, freshly shorn, had arisen from the grass, paired with another youth groupie. Reily and the girl poked his way.

Wil corralled his friend and pointed at the run. "I think this feeds into the side creek, the one where we catch the natives." He nudged his chin toward the newfound fishery. "You won't believe what you see."

Reily followed orders and saw what Wil saw. "I never knew."

"It's what they call a revelation."

The girl squealed, interrupting veneration. She pointed wide-eyed and frizzy-haired. "There's a copperhead, right there."

Along the base of the limestone wall of the springhouse laid a small snake, mottled brown and white, attempting to bask in the final rays of the day.

Wil scooped it into his hands, to the girl's horror. "It's a milk snake. Harmless." He had found his object for show and tell.

Reily tailed him back to the courtyard. "I see you got your head chopped, too."

"Yep, yesterday after school." Wil hated haircuts, although he could see much better. He felt lighter, too. With three or more inches now gone, Reily might float away, but his friend's pelt remained uncontrollable. Nevertheless, their conformity quotient *had* improved.

Other kids presented rocks, flowers, and leaves for their samples of wonder and beauty. Only Wil had a live serpent, gauging its handler with incredulity.

The pastor grinned. "*They will pick up serpents with their hands—* Mark, chapter 16."

Wil held it high for all to see.

The snake drew inordinate attention, which the cleric seized for additional pontification. "Snakes are referenced throughout the Bible, often as being emblematic of the Devil, but terms like 'clever' and even 'wise' are also used to describe them. In John 3, Moses lifts up a serpent in the wilderness, like our friend Wil."

Wil ignored the prophet comparison, and scooted off with the pastor's blessing to return the creature to its rightful home. He thought of the snakes along the Mannequin. Were they "clever" enough to stop a colossally stupid project?

On the walk back, he saw Reily, trimmed and dawdling amongst the others, doing his best to rise above Colleen-induced chaos. Wil owed him extra thanks for his crazed, but effective heroics the prior weekend. Troy didn't know what hit him, but it still gnawed at Wil.

I should have stood up for myself.

Say of the Day: atonement.

48

Angling required composure, deliberation—behaviors familiar to Boom, although he feared they would be usurped by eagerness. He evaluated the spinning reel and fiberglass pole, on loan from Reily, clutched in his left hand. *Generous Reily.* Behind him, footsteps in the leaves verified the preoccupied presence of two friends, one searching amongst the trees.

"The tree can wait," Eddie protested. "The Fish Commission stocked palominos at the bridge." Eddie carried his fishing rod upright, like a holy staff in the hands of a ruffian. "I'll try and leave some for you two, but no guarantees." He spat on the ground and marched away.

"There it is." Reily's outburst made Boom jump. "See the big oak?"

"It is impossible to miss." The living monument stood above all others. "I know this tree, too." Boom had seen the beast before on training runs. *The stand back tree.* Younger trees cowered, yielding deferential space.

Reily jogged toward it, dropped his duffel, and dug for a prize inside. "Yes," he decreed, wielding a tape measurer.

Boom watched, amused. "What are you doing?" Reily failed to answer.

"Give me a hand." Reily lent the end of the tape to Boom. "Get right up to it. Lean close." Boom abided as Reily shimmied around the hulk of the tree, releasing a metal ribbon. Knots dressed scaly bark flecked tan and gray. A gaping void at its base doubled as an apartment for a raccoon or opossum. The lowest limb, a brute twice as round as most of the trees nearby, split off twelve feet above the ground, reaching for the lowering sun. Acorn fragments scattered outward, as if detonated. Fresh, round-lobed leaves hung by the thousands.

Reily's gauging hand arrived next to his. "Holy crap. I got twenty-three feet, two inches."

"That is big, yes."

The flannel-attired, budding botanist gawked with effervescing glee. "Gigantic. It might be the largest white oak in Pennsylvania."

"We should check again."

At the same height, a second measurement returned the same result. "I knew it was a special tree, but not this special." Reily held up his long arms for a final approximation of girth. "There's all kinds of folklore and mystery about oaks. They're legendary. Everlasting. I like how white oaks in particular hang on to their dead leaves through winter. It's as if they are afraid to let go."

Boom laughed. "Long live the tree."

Eddie yelled from afar, words distorted, ignorant to the science at work.

Reily hid the measuring tape in his pack and scribbled notes on a pad. "We better catch up with Eddie before he scares all the fish."

Two hours of daylight remained. The weather column in the newspaper printed the time of sunset and sunrise, and the level of the Lehigh River. The height of the river related to the amount of recent rainfall, suggesting the trail through the woods on the other side of the creek would be too soggy for a run. Boom liked the deductive process he had begun to employ. Knowledge gave one a leg up.

Reily navigated them toward the water. "Is it true there's a new track star at West Bethlehem?"

"I'm not sure, but it is a good sport. Quite enjoyable. Three of us placed one, two, and three in the mile last week."

"That's impressive. Where did you come in?"

"Second place . . . one second behind Mr. You-Know-Who."

Reily had a satisfied look. "The king better watch out—he's about to be dethroned."

"Ha, I don't know. He is fast." A branch scratched Boom's arm, affirming his vulnerability. He believed it always best to be humble. "Troy has spoken a few words and short sentences to me. 'Ben, get over here.' 'Ben, stay in your lane.' At least, I know he can speak, or should I say still speak, after his, umm, corrective punishment."

Reily shook his head. "Very funny, but he'll be speechless when he loses."

A disheveled angler straddled rocks before them.

"Where have you losers been?" One of Eddie's cheeks protruded in the shape of an orb.

Reily scowled in disapproval. "Don't tell me you're chewing tobacco?"

"It's been awhile. So are you two going to fish or stand there?" Eddie motioned to a fallen sycamore covered in small sticks and debris, lying parallel to the shore, the water slack in front of it. "I had a nice strike by that log."

Reily placed his things on a different log. Out came a plastic box with the proper ingredients for fishing—hooks, weights, and lures in smaller plastic boxes. "I think I'll start you with bait, but I want you to try a spinner, too."

"You are the expert." Boom admired the variety and graduated sizes of items.

"Dang it." Undistracted by their arrival, Eddie continued the hunt. "That cold-blooded lowlife stole another worm."

"Let Boom have a chance at it." Reily tied a tiny hook to the end of the line as if he were tying toy shoes. "There. All set. Eddie, throw me a worm."

Eddie plunged his fingers in a cardboard container—the kind used for takeout food. He found a suitable earthworm and made an underhand pitch.

Reily caught the flying worm and handed it to Boom. "I'll let you put it on the hook."

Boom became a surgeon, devoid of empathy, piercing the wriggling patient twice as it struggled to evade torture in sacrifice for a higher purpose. Soil particles peppered his skin.

Reily made a demo cast with the self-assurance of an outdoorsman on a TV show. He retrieved the line and passed the equipment to Boom. "Give it a try."

His first attempt smacked the worm on a rock, adding insult to the invertebrate's injuries. The next cast made it to water shallow enough to be the worm's bathtub.

Eddie lost interest in the spectacle and trudged upstream, making muddy rivulets with careless steps.

It took two more tries, but Boom finally reached the target. He inhaled in triumph, relishing life in the swampy surroundings. "Now what should I do?"

Reily gave his shoulder a congratulatory squeeze. "Reel slowly."

Boom did. Nothing happened. The exercise repeated, and repeated again. By the tenth cast, Boom questioned his methods.

Reily read his mind. "Don't worry, you're doing fine. Fishing is a slow business." He sidestepped to the log, stretched out, and pretended to nap. "Wake me up when you have a bite."

The repetition of angling had a strange appeal. Like a cat stalking a bird, nothing else mattered. Furtive concentration. Minutes turned to an hour. Boom's only catch: a stubborn crayfish clamped to his fifth worm.

Reily resurrected. "Time to use the spinner." He affixed a yellow, feathered widget called a rooster tail and advised Boom to try another hole of his choosing. "Cast and retrieve, but not too fast. Don't let it touch bottom or it will snag."

"Got it. Good instructions." Boom evaluated the options. The creek ran straight at this point, the bridge visible in the distance. Halfway there, the surface slackened. Upstream, Eddie stalked, immersed in a knee-deep basin. Reily returned to the log. His long torso seemed made to meditate upon the matters of life, happy or sad.

In position, Boom marveled at the transparency of the emerald liquid surrounding him. Cobbled bottom tapered to darker lairs. Cast. Recovery. He mastered the procedure with ease. Something rose, piercing the interface between two worlds. Boom put the next cast behind the epicenter and reeled. The line tightened, pulled, and pulsed. He cranked with fervor until a submarine—golden and pink—bumped against the old sneakers on his feet. Boom lifted the fish with wet hands. The lure hung at its lip. Unsure of how to remove the contraption, he bit the line, revering the splendor inches away. Without a stringer, transportation would be complicated, but Boom had an ingenious idea.

He splashed toward his friends.

"Any luck?" Reily had the look of someone who had overslept. "Why are you grinning so much?"

Eddie stood there too, eyeing him with suspicion. "You caught something, didn't you?"

Boom expanded with pride. "Yes. I did."

"Well, where is it?" Eddie could be quite impatient.

Boom unzipped his windbreaker and spread it open, as if selling contraband. "Right here." From an inner pocket twitched the caudal fin of a palomino trout.

The upside-down fish surely found scant amusement in its dilemma, but Reily and Eddie collapsed in riotous laughter.

Empty stomachs drew them homeward in fading slants of sun. The sluff through the woods cultivated talk of a fishing jacket prototype. The *Kabumba Expeditioner* would have not one, but six odor-absorbent, reinforced inner slots for storing the day's catch. The millions of dollars made would go to the establishment of Mannequin Creek National Park—the latest, greatest addition to America's fabled holdings.

49

Merle jostled competing emotions as he toured the hydro site in clumsy, rubberized boots. Evelyn Darkes would have made it to ninety if not for choking on an unpitted prune. Blues induced by Mom's celestial departure dragged him into a dark void chiseled deeper by a surprise donation mandated in her will—a gift to the anti-development Pinelands Preservation Alliance. His mother never set foot in the Pine Barrens of New Jersey, or touched nature in any form. Even her houseplants were imitations. However, a male admirer at the retirement village regaled his captive with vintage photos of canoeing forays through sand and muck, and exaggerated accounts of personal involvement in victory over a proposal to build the world's largest jetport in the middle of needleleaf paradise. Nostalgic enthusiasm unleashed uncommon benevolence in Evelyn, and reduced Merle's net inheritance.

Ebullience returned by redirecting his immediate thoughts to the state's decision. He had license to proceed, at least from this band of pious regulators. A favorite sentence from the certified letter scrolled in his shrewd, calculating mind: "While the black racer (*Coluber constrictor*) and rough green snake (*Opheodrys aestivus*) are candidate threatened species and listed threatened species, respectively, we have no evidence of their occurrence on the lands within the project boundaries."

Upwards Merle writhed in short, awkward steps. Field season meant exertion. Exertion brought weight loss. He had shed two pounds in the past two weeks. Bearing a firmer, fitter frame, his secretary might ask *him* out.

He reached the creek, a lifeline to a richer livelihood. The stream sparkled in submission. The leaflets of a young ash fluttered at his side, proof that even the trees praised his domination. Merle gazed upon the subject and it moved again. A sentient green cord turned on a branch in deft, coiling contractions. He thought of pythons and death by constriction, the inability to suck in oxygen—a taste of poor Mom's last gasps. The puny varmint spanned a foot at best, and, Merle guessed, must be incapable of crushing a grown man . . . *but was it venomous?*

An urgent, greater fear arose—one of recognition. The snake seemed satiny, *but might it be the consequential, coarse variety?* If seeing meant believing, then he bore witness to something he should not see . . . not here, *please not here.* His brain said, "Ignore," as it did regarding the bones the consultants found, and the cremated remains of his uninterred mother.

Merle left the outlaw viper behind like a bad dream and conjured peppy thoughts of roaring water, smiling visitors, and servile investors. Three skidders materialized along a remnant road—biblical Goliaths ready to scrape away burdensome vermin with indisputable efficiency upon his command. *Let the eradication begin.*

50

The phone jangled, disrupting an ancient episode of *The Monkees*. Eddie guessed it might be Reily and almost made a fart sound into the receiver. To his surprise, a woman asked for Edward Knisely. The person spewed unforeseen news. A young man with his name had won first place in the youth watercolors category at the Hellertown Arts Festival.

Not since first grade had Eddie bounced on a bed, but now the mattress had become a stand-in for clouds. He tested the limits of box spring integrity, rebounding at will to Led Zeppelin's "Misty Mountain Hop" on maximum volume and risking toppling his growing collection of beer cans. Mrs. Watters had encouraged him to enter his artwork into the contest and Rachel helped him deliver it. Reily's mom believed the piece "captured the essence of Mannequin Creek." The judges must have agreed. The portrayal of the loch included a tree carved with initials. In the original sketch, he scribed EK+RW, but feared Rachel's reaction. He came up with a better idea: WW+KB—Wil's love story captured for years to come. Troy Troxell would rupture if he ever saw the painting, although the jughead probably couldn't comprehend cultural stuff.

More or less everyone came to the Saturday reception, or so it seemed to Eddie. Rachel simmered in a short-cut dress. Reily had another date with a canoe and a river, but his mother arrived early, spouting rave reviews about her art student to all in attendance. She brought along Keith Watters, notably thinner but continually bronzed from too much time at Florida Air Force bases. He scrutinized each piece of art as if inspecting an F-4 before a mission. Wil's parents were there, too. Mr. Wiz played with his tie, his hands bored when freed from a chassis. Next to the hors d'oeuvres, Mrs. Wiz spread out a platter of cookies as chunky as her midsection. Wil supposedly hurt his ankle playing basketball and needed to rest it at home. Likely story. Kelly had to be at his side, aiding recuperation with body heat therapy. Other than his flakey best friends, the one notable absence belonged to Earl Knisely. Eddie knew not to expect much from his father, certainly not appearing at an art show—even if his son had received an award.

The room stirred with the adult sounds of ice clinking into glasses and hushed conversation. While the grownups mingled and munched, Rachel led him to a corner.

"I'm the art history person, and here I am with a soon to be legendary artist." She nudged him for fun with her shoulder. "Not bad work, Eddie."

He wanted the two of them to head to his house for a jumping-on-the-bed session, but a tap on a mic startled the lot. He checked his watch. Two o'clock. His nerves tingled. The remarks began.

Eddie scanned the space, rehearsing an acceptance handshake. A mirage crystallized, a man in off-color slacks with a face hollowed by bitterness: Earl Knisely in the flesh.

An amplified voice summoned Eddie. With his head sagging from mortification, he shook hands with the people gathered around the podium and in one gleeful grasp, accepted a check for seventy-five dollars.

Inconspicuous again in the modest crowd, a firm pat on the back startled him. Eddie wheeled to find Pop, with the unfamiliar gleam of a tomcat delivering a mouse on a platter.

The pride, or whatever fueled his father, morphed the lone ranger into a social dude. For the first time in years, he jabbered away with Wil's dad and Mr. Watters. The more they spoke, the closer they leaned, as if conspiring over dirty jokes, but they were not laughing.

Eddie appraised his winnings. Across the room, hovering like a superstar, Rachel guarded the punchbowl. He would drink scorched motor oil for that girl. She motioned him over. He pocketed the check, dreaming of ways to spend it.

51

Newly licensed, Reily drove for the Delaware River, considering the blessings and curses of inevitability. The Colleen annulment may have been predestined, a rational outcome of a circumstantial progression: school, hormones, attraction, and distraction. Telephone silence had reached fifteen days. Conversation quality had shrunk proportionally with call frequency. Headaches must be contagious, because hers became his by the conclusion of their word-weary chats. The self-imposed punishment ended on Colleen's confession—without penitence—of a new friend of the saliva-swapping variety, the one and only gridiron Kyle. Reily's comeback lacked profundity and cheer: "Have a swell summer."

In comparison, chance connections on a river, and in a store, catalyzed the forthcoming outing—the kind of quest that could purge many problems. Life hurts, but it also heals . . . depending on its temperament.

In contrast, Wil's demise, or emancipation, depending on perspective, struck like a tuna in freshwater, or so he said. Certainly, to all involved, it seemed *less* inevitable than the dissolution Reily had experienced. After a physical "session"—as Wil referenced adoring sprees with Kelly—she nonchalantly suggested a need to "broaden her field." Wil, attempting a sardonic, agricultural analogy, asked if she were some sort of hoe. Kelly interpreted his use of the term in a pejorative context. Things escalated. Mr. Sturdy turned to mush in Ms. Bingham's departing wake.

Reily fixated on the road ahead and flexed his grip on the steering wheel. Motorized wheels replaced pedals and feet. Anywhere had become possible. The simple and familiar contracted as the map expanded. A golf cart became a comic book insect on a country club golf course with felt green fairways. Farms aligned shipshape and tidy with cows and corn in alternating fields. Frisky, fair weather clouds speckled a limitless dome of sky. Marveling at the curiosities, he almost missed the turn for Lower Mud Run Road.

Steve Patterson, grown-up Boy Scout, stood ready at the side of the ramp, two canoes at his feet. Reily eased into a parking space next to Steve's truck, an International Harvester bearing stickers of wish list parks and exceptional places. The rest of the spaces were empty.

"Today, we're each going solo." Steve pointed at the pair of tapered boats, shorter than tandems. "Are you good with that?"

Reily admired a navy hull with gunwales of pale, polished wood. "Can I take the blue one?"

Steve laughed. "I guess that's a yes. She's all yours, but first we have to set up the shuttle. Follow me to Easton."

Reily obliged, keeping the decorated pickup in close visual reach. After fifteen minutes, Steve eased into the entrance road of a shady city park and ducked into an end spot, as if reserved only for him. A hundred feet away, a liquid conveyor belt moved at a funeral pace, without hurry or worry.

On the way back to the boat launch, Steve went over what to expect. Reily half-listened, preoccupied by the river gorge, civil but wild, with steep bluffs cloaked in leafy, burgeoning summer coats. A rapid here, an island there. Gentle bends curving out of sight. Downstream, a hundred miles or more, a prearranged union with the sea. Supreme inevitability at its best.

52

William "Billy" Tilghman skimmed the papers on his lap, pausing as needed to fend off nausea. The details of the report and the motion of the car competed to make him queasy. His assistant steered like a drunk, but retained details like a tape recorder.

The obedient sycophant—runt of the family litter—contrasted with his own bombastic mass. As Chief Commissioner of the Federal Power Commission, Billy had reached an apex in his thirty-year government career. Coasting toward retirement, he obsessed over previous decisions. Too often, he had acquiesced to the political currents, allowing principles to fall victim to expediency.

Now he approached his work with a brazen new attitude, an emboldened who-gives-a-crap way of doing business. Soon enough, he would be chasing stripers full-time in his Bayliner—if the Bay didn't go belly-up in the interim. For generations, the Chesapeake abundantly gave to the Tilghmans. The future of the estuary—and every waterway for that matter—deserved to be foremost in all deliberations.

"Sir, may I ask why you want to see this project site?"

Junior had interrupted important thoughts. "I think I've earned the right to inspect a site when I want to. Or do you disagree?" Billy got a kick from watching underlings squirm. "Keep your eyes peeled for the interstate."

"Yes, of course. I simply wondered if you are concerned about what's been proposed."

"It's our job to be concerned. We are *not* an economic development agency." He spied a crane putting up another half-ass high rise along the

Baltimore-Washington Parkway. His employee strained to read a sign, tuning out the coming rant. "That is how we're viewed though. We are the yes-men . . . pawns in the pockets of the powerful."

"Do you have any questions about the project? I've read the entire docket—" The subordinate swerved to catch an on-ramp.

Billy hung on. "I'm sure you have." His rural Maryland twang made the dig sound a bit too harsh. He placed his immense arm behind the driver's headrest and chuckled. "I'm glad you've gone through it, because I've only read the first twenty pages."

"Everything seems in order."

Of course it does. Anyone could bullshit through an application, no matter how oppressive the mound of paperwork. Early morning beltway traffic congealed like algae on a pond. Billy popped two Tums. "Maybe I'm getting soft, but I want to determine what's going down, live and in-person. I like to meet the parties, too . . . look 'em in the eyes and see what they're made of." He whacked the back of the nervous driver. "Know what I'm sayin'?"

The driver straightened. "Yes, sir. I think I do."

Children cannot learn when the toilets cannot flush, Reily mused over morning waffles, pools of syrup symbolic of a flooded school. Thanks to a broken pipe, the high school had no water. Lucky Monday.

On the floor, Marlin sampled the ether, nose in the air, sensing food and after-breakfast intentions. "Yes boy, don't worry, we'll go to the creek."

At eleven, Reily called Wil. He knew not to try any earlier. The jarring ring of the Wisnoski phone ruined all slumber. "Get up, you drugged koala."

"I think I have rigor mortis."

"A free day is wasting."

Wil yawned as if auditioning for a sleeping contest. "Give me an hour."

Despite his prolonged dormancy, Wil showed a little past noon. A brief debate ensued—basketball or fishing. Fishing won. Nary an angler came to the Mannequin on a weekday.

On the front porch, they met Boom, wet with sweat and breathing like an accordion. "I ran here," he mumbled, hands on his hips.

"We couldn't tell." Wil had a tackle box in one hand, a rod in the other, and mockery in the mind.

"You want to come with us?" Reily motioned with own his tackle, nearly hooking Boom.

"Yes. Thank you. Of course." Even out of breath, Boom sounded dignified.

Together, they left the Watters's land and passed the former Kemp Farm. Wil walked backwards and gave the site a dejected glance. "It's a shadow of its former self." A cardinal bellowed three times, before punctuating the stanza with three short notes. The message repeated, then appropriately silenced, as they exited the ghost town—still, dusty, and depressing.

Reily contemplated the decimation. "They blocked the light."

Boom furrowed his forehead. "What do you mean *blocked?*"

"A shadow is an area of darkness, right?"

Wil scanned Reily head to toe. "Have you been hitting Eddie's bottle?"

"I'm serious." Reily disapproved of the ill-timed levity. "They took an area of goodness, land that made food for people and had nooks for fish and other animals, and they made it bad. They took away the good, the light . . . they blocked it out."

Boom tipped his head up and down, processing the statement.

Wil, and his lady-charming chin, retained a stupid smile which Reily pretended to ignore, but Wil kept at his side. "Nooks?"

"Keep walking, heathen."

Before they reached the bridge, they saw an odd sight: men in business clothes talking in the woods. Suit jackets in the soggy bottomlands seemed downright dumb and out of place. Reily steered his crew away from the polyester invaders, but a sizeable member of the overdressed entourage waved them over.

"What are you young fellas up to? It's a school day, isn't it?" The man had the appearance of a gambler in an old Western.

"No sir, we have the day off. Our school had a water problem." For some reason, the man chuckled at the explanation and glanced at the two others in his party. One beady-eyed, goose-legged man looked familiar. The third guy—a younger man—had a sad, confused expression, as if he would rather be a thousand miles away.

"I take it you fellas like to fish?" said the big man.

"Yes, we fish here a lot." Reily tagged him as the talkative type.

"You don't say. What do you catch?"

Wil stepped forward. "Mostly brown trout and rainbow trout. Upstream, sometimes wild brooks. Downstream, they also stock palominos."

"Ah, golden rainbows." The man moved his giant head up and down. "Sounds like a fine stream." He turned to skinny legs. "You're planning to pump from the river, but that's warm water. How do the trout feel about that?"

Before the human wading bird could respond, Reily pegged his identity: *the dam developer*.

The quack stuttered, attempting an answer. "The temperature differential is modest. We are confident that storage dynamics, mixing, and residency intervals will mitigate extremes."

"That's a ton of turds, Merle." The big man glared at the alleged liar. "The fish are adjusted to a constant, cold shower, but you'll be giving them a warm bathtub with a leaky drain. They won't be happy."

The younger member of the anomalous trio opened a notebook. "Sir, the application has data to back Mr. Darkes's assertions."

The large man slapped the younger man on the back, causing the latter's glasses to plop to the ground. "That's impressive. Didn't you ever read *How to Lie with Statistics*?" The smacker crossed his arms and set his jaws in a cynical grimace. "And what about the discharge? That's a lot of water to push through that stream channel."

"Our plans included hardening portions of the banks and bed with concrete." Darkes spit his words, agitated and defensive.

The large man shook his head with doubt and gazed at Reily, Wil, and Boom. "What do you boys think?"

The forest stood still. For once, an adult asked for youths' opinions. Reily prepared to respond, but Boom stole the moment. "If I understand how this will function, then it is, indeed, a poor idea, sir. The stream has many fish and this valley," Boom swept his arm in deference to the geography, "is full of wild things that should be left untrammeled."

Reily and Wil checked one another. *Did he just say untrammeled?*

The heron-like developer winced. The younger man scanned for corroborating pages in a pathetic report. The big man simply grinned. "That's a heck of a vocabulary you have there."

"Thank you, sir." Boom radiated like the sun. "May we show you something?"

The heron inched forward. "I'm afraid we have other sites to visit."

"Now Merle, I think the fellas want to give their own show and tell. You wait your turn." The big man nodded to Boom. "Where did you want to take us?"

Boom grew another inch. "To a very special tree."

Impeccable timing, Boom. The men accompanying the developer must be government people. Reily seized the moment. "You can all follow me." He led them the short distance to the white oak and the tree appeared, immovable and unshakable. Manna along the Mannequin.

The beefy man circled in awe. "Why I'll be . . . how big is she?"

Reily rattled off the specs. "I think it may be a new state champion."

The heron seemed to shrink, as if a hungry snapper gnawed off his feet at the ankles.

"You don't say." The hulking government man extended a mitt. "I'm Bill Tilghman, Federal Power Commission. And you are . . ."

"Reily Watters . . . arbiter of the wilderness, and this is Boom and Wil."

A smirk grew on Bill's ruddy face. "Arbiter, huh. Well, what else can y'all tell me?"

They had the commissioner's attention. Boom delivered an exposé on the snake situation and Wil regaled him with fish tales.

In the leaf litter, Reily glimpsed a washed-out subscription card from a *Playboy* magazine. A woman in lingerie gave a naughty, approving wink, and the land smiled in exultation. Nature had the final word . . . *the tree of life.*

53

Wil straddled the courtside bench at Weyant Park for what may have been the thousandth time. While Reily obsessed and dallied, he soaked in the scene. Through the years, it had changed little. Same lights. Same fence. Same lumpy asphalt. Only he and Reily had transformed, proved by the scratchy stubble sprouting on his own face.

Wil assessed the basketball before him. "This thing is done. A potato has more bounce." He heard a hiss.

Reily scraped a pebble against the playing surface like a bored preschooler. "Maybe it's angry."

"The inflation port is shot." Wil catapulted the ball into the field. "I'll get it later."

"You have two more balls."

"Very funny, Watters. Actually, I have three. I chose the wrong one . . . like falling for Kelly."

"You have to snap out of it. *We* have to snap out of it."

"You had months to prepare. A bomb was dropped on me." Reily had it right. Time to cease the fixation and divert. "Did you hear about the creek stuff?"

"What now?" Reily tossed the pebble up in the air and caught it.

"My dad told me, and he seemed pissed when he said it . . . the state gave the approval."

Reily began pacing the court. "That's not fair."

"I know, but the federal people still have to weigh in. There's a chance it won't happen."

"Nobody cares." Reily laid down in the center circle and stared into the glow above.

"You're supposed to be the optimist, flannel boy. Aren't you hot in that?" Reily had chopped off the sleeves, but now the shirt and its wearer had hillbilly qualities.

Reily sat bolt upright. "We could make explosives if we have to. Blow up stuff. Eddie will know how. God is on our side."

"Wait a minute, G.I. Joe. That's a little extreme, even by my standards. Let's just wait and see."

Reily went prone again, and silent.

Wil tried another diversion. "How's your dad feeling? He seemed better last time I saw him."

"Okay, I guess." Reily grunted from the macadam. "He went bowling tonight. He hasn't done that for a long time."

"That's weird. My dad went bowling tonight, too." The shoes his father used when he "rolled" were last seen gathering mildew in a damp corner of the garage.

"Well, at least those balls don't leak."

Wil chased Reily to the car.

Tangy air rushed through the windows on the ride home. It felt cool, but strange to be riding beside Reily in the front seat, especially with him at the controls. Adulthood, or something akin to it, had snuck up on them. The car had more horsepower than a thousand Schwinns and the ability to go far, but bikes were a part of them—dependable, utilitarian members of the gang. Now the two-wheelers were destined for neglect. Outcasts soon to be forgotten.

The car jerked to a stop at the Wisnoski abode. "Thanks for the lift, Watters."

"Talk to you soon," Reily muttered.

Wil watched the taillights until they vanished . . . like the fleeting routines of the past.

Say of the Day: uncharted.

Reily pulled into the driveway and maneuvered Mom's car to its rightful spot. Dad's sedan remained absent. Reily worried. His father's skin tone and stamina had not fully returned. Bowling seemed risky for a man with a healing heart.

Once inside, Marlin pounced. The brown-eyed beast had learned the click of the back door deadbolt and waylaid the unsuspecting with an energetic tongue bath. They play wrestled on the floor for several slobbery moments before Reily placated him with a bacon flavored treat.

Mom had the television on, but devoted her attention to a novel about an art heist in London. Cities were okay, and Reily liked art, but the book advertised boring. Nothing this evening garnered much of his interest.

In his bedroom, Reily turned on the radio and prepped his backpack for school, feeding it textbooks. The final weeks of bio explored the human body—the cardiovascular system, the anatomy of the brain, and the reproductive system. *What a way to end the year.*

Bodies made him think of Colleen—the misguided beauty with the capable mind, if only put to better use. The changes in store for the Mannequin were another misguided mess. He placed a pillow over his head and muffled a scream. His heart needed hardening. Less feeling, more indifference.

The newest issue of *National Geographic* offered a half hour respite to the turquoise waters of Spain's Balearic Islands and an account of the recent Lake Superior sinking of the Edmund Fitzgerald. Reily stifled a bear-sized yawn, tiring from the mental journey.

Marlin paid a gregarious visit with ulterior motives of nighttime escapades and bladder relief. Reily capitulated, found the leash by the water bowl, and exited to star-filled firmaments. Although unable to vocalize complex thoughts, his four-legged pal somehow communicated a shared appreciation for planetary wonders . . . and the simple gift of an evening adventure.

Marlin pulled him down the driveway, heading for a preferred tree to soak. Headlights startled them.

Keith Watters rolled down a window. "How are my boys?"

"Pretty good, I guess." Reily knew best to sound cheery, or else face further scrutiny. "How was bowling?"

Dad hesitated. "Not bad. My game is a little rusty, but we had fun."

"I was starting to worry about you. Does the doctor mind you doing stuff like that?"

"Like what?" Dad seemed awkward—apprehensive, defensive, or both. "Bowling? Sure. It's not a very arduous sport."

"Just you and Wil's dad went?"

"Mr. Knisley came along, too."

Reily almost dropped the leash. "Really? Eddie's dad? He's always a grump."

"He was great. Earl knows his stuff." The engine whinnied. "The fan belt's going. I'll see you inside." The car rolled forward.

Reily let Marlin take him further out the lane. The silly dog pushed his snout into the brush, probing at random for anything dead or alive. Reily sifted his own curiosities. Something didn't smell right about bowling, and Dad seldom conversed with Eddie's father, let alone hung out with him.

Back inside, Reily reached for a towel on the peg hanger behind the door. Mom had trained him to always wipe Marlin's paws upon reentry. Below, on the floor, sat Dad's dark leather shoes, clotted with mud. A weird state for the footwear of a fastidious man who went to the lanes on a dry evening.

54

Eddie felt foreign at West Bethlehem's stadium. He looked at it the bulk of the year, but seldom seated himself in the stands. Spectating, especially at a track meet, offered little stimulation . . . except when Rachel made him do it. His liaisons with her continued unscathed. A shared nonchalance gave rise to occasional smooch fests—sometimes spontaneous, always electrifying.

These days, the lives of Reily and Wil lacked any such spark, their babe batteries drained and dead. Campout plans survived the breakups, but if Eddie had to hear Wil whine one more time about Kelly the garden hoe, he might puke. Commemorating the approaching end of the school year and start of summer gave ample motivation for the bivouac. Fear of ruination of the lands along the Mannequin made them persevere. They might not be *able* to camp there in the future. The horrendous thought made him shudder.

The stakes were high for the creek and their buddy Boom, stretching on the turf. Bishop Mallory's lineup included the notorious Kyle—Colleen's heart thief and bowlegged hurdler. Mallory, also known as BM or the Friars, held first place in the division standings, with West Bethlehem right behind. Success in the long-distance events depended on Boom and Troy the idiot Troxell, if he could refrain from attacking his own team member.

Eddie felt a repetitive bump on his shoulder. He spied Reily ready to strike again with his forehead. "What's wrong with you? Are you having a seizure or something?"

"She's over there. Second row. At the end." Reily, resembling a mangy, orphaned coyote, nudged his head at the opposing bleachers.

Eddie picked out Colleen's crow-colored hair and stubby but sizzling structure. "Don't worry, Jethro." He shook his goggling friend. "She probably saw you, too, and is thinking 'why did I ditch him for the boy with frog legs?'"

Reily failed to find humor in the comment. He slung his head, no doubt pleading for a private go-around the track with Colleen or a javelin accident making a Kyle kebab.

As Reily grappled with dejection, Kelly Bingham prowled the grounds with her saucy, sable mane. Wil rose to his feet and wobbled, like a stressed robotic teddy bear, and staggered out of the stands. He needed more self-respect, and less time with the high school tease.

"Where's he going?" Eddie mouthed the question to Rachel. She tossed up her arms.

Track meets, being a slow affair, allowed time for Rachel to go in search of Wil. Reily came to life, and waved over Cindy, the walking stick, there to pull for Boom on the big day. Eddie watched the weather. Storm clouds were brewing.

After a few sprints, eight runners prepared for the 120-yard hurdles. Colleen's Kyle had the innermost lane.

Eddie jumped at the snap of the starting gun. Kyle took the lead with two WB kids a hair behind. On the final hurdle, one of Kyle's shifty ankles clipped the cross piece and he went down, collecting souvenir cinders on his kneecaps.

Eddie checked Reily for signs of gloating, but the peacekeeper remained sullen. Rachel returned, towing Wil, the temporary basket case. Boom offered distraction, readying for the 880-yard relay and retying his shoes.

The race caused heart stoppage, each leg a dragster sprint. Boom gave Troy a flawless handoff of the baton and the super jock took it home.

Boom walked off the victory and waved a greeting to his fans. Eddie raised a salutary fist. Troy, the former assailant, gave a distinct nod, an honest-to-God acknowledgment to his prior victim. Eddie thought he heard thunder.

The Friars ran for papal glory in the mile, the victory putting them ahead in total points. The two-miler became the deciding race. Boom stretched beside Troy, district record holder in that very event. Two string beans from Mallory goofed around, undaunted. WB needed this one. Eddie fidgeted on the cool metal of the bleacher bench. He became surprisingly aware that he actually cared who won. But first, the bathroom commanded a visit.

Upon his return to the stands, Eddie saw Boom on the outside, striding like an elk in rut, with his head held high. Troy, as usual, led the pack.

"Is Boom smiling?" Cindy said, showing her own gleaming whites.

"He never stops," Reily answered, eyes focused on the subject.

By the sixth lap, Eddie and his four oddball friends stood breathless. Boom surged to within a few yards of Troy. The two Friars appeared fried, but Boom evidently had more than a meet on his mind. Entering lap seven, Troy quickened. Boom did, too. He slowly edged parallel with Troy as if they planned to stroll across the finish line hand in hand. Troy's face protested, but Boom found a secret gear. Overdrive.

Boom won it by a yard. The seizure of first and second place sealed West Bethlehem's victory. Better yet, Boom had upset the district champ, today downgraded to district *chump*. In celebration, Eddie and his offbeat crew mobbed the infield.

Boom stood before them, kickass lord of the track, laughing, trying to spit out words as Cindy squeezed him.

Reily gave Boom a friendly jostle. "What did you say?"

Eddie leaned in to hear the response, regretting his judgmental idiocy of months past. Boom was a solid dude. A real decent person.

Boom shone with a supersized grin, and answered, "The black racer wins the day."

The sky released an ominous reverberation that sounded like God calling the victor by name. Troy appeared dumbstruck.

Eddie administered a Dutch rub to the top of Boom's head. Troy came forward and extended a hand to his teammate, adding more strangeness to the crazy cauldron of emotions.

Boom shook it like a maraca. "I heard you have a scholarship to Montclair State for football. Good luck."

"Thanks." Troxell said it gruffly, monotone.

Truce achieved. Nixon and China. Eddie nodded Troy's direction. Reily and Wil followed his lead.

Yahweh crashed the party. A big, gusty breath blew heavy splatters of raindrops, causing the stadium to regurgitate occupants clambering for cover.

Eddie went for grub. His boys fell in line behind him, seeking a free meal. Reily carried the doping sting of Colleen. Wil wore Kelly-angst like a weird California fashion. The drumming of water on the galvanized roof composed a soundtrack for the funeral procession to the food concession.

From the littered shadows beneath the angled stands, a hobbled, sodden, cutthroat Kyle emerged and stuck an elbow into Reily's back. Reily moaned and reached for the lumbar region. The sneaky BMer pretended the assault was accidental. His acting sucked, but it brought to life the walking dead. Before Eddie could administer pain, Wil plowed Kyle backwards into the wall. Pinned against cinder blocks painted a bleak shade of gray, the sore loser hurdled protests. Wil told him to shush and offered explicit advice.

"Never touch my friend again. Never. Understand?"

Kyle, nodding reluctantly, morphed from manly man to mouse. Wil had the rodent trapped, but, in mercy, granted him release.

The offender scurried off, tail between his legs. A bearded teacher, Kreider the bio-man, observed the application of justice, shook his head, and said nothing. Wil composed himself and returned to the roughshod line.

Reily touted a half-assed smile in honor of Wisnoski. "Thanks for saving *my* back."

Eddie dismissed the interruption to their eventful afternoon at the track, and salivated at a passing mound of fries. Someday he hoped to eat french fries in Paris with his college-bound sweetie, although he refused to learn the language. *What will my pathetic posse do without me when art fame takes me overseas?*

55

After a Friday morning call, Merle dabbed tears, sniffling like a barnyard hog in the wood-paneled corral that was his office. In a three-to-two decision, the Federal Power Commission denied Eastern Power a permit for a pumped storage hydroelectric dam on the Mannequin Creek in Northampton County, Pennsylvania. William Tilghman cast the tie-breaking vote.

The Commission's minion relayed the grim facts. Consultation with U.S. Fish and Wildlife Service biologists had compared habitat types with species distribution, deeming black racer and rough green snake populations to be of high probability in the project area. The minion also cited the Chief Commissioner's oratory about an outstanding specimen of *Quercus alba*—the white oak deserving of preservation and recognition.

Merle became dizzy. He loosened his tie and unfastened his belt, recalling more of the dismissal . . . "Probable water temperature spikes in discharge water pose unacceptable risks to downstream fauna." *They didn't take a single, godforsaken measurement.* "Erratic flow regimes are likely to cause severe erosion downstream and deposition in receiving waters." He bowed his head, touching forehead to desk, pleading for intercession on the altar of enterprise.

The secretary slid her head through the ajar office door. "You okay? There's another call for you."

Merle motioned for her to send it through. *Anything to take my mind off this calamity.*

The field manager of the heavy equipment leasing company identified himself. "Merle, we have a problem."

What could be worse than the prior call?

"Someone, or a bunch of someones, messed up the dozers and movers. They're missing bolts and engine parts. They also detached a couple of the blades." The man's tone of speech implied that Merle shared blame.

"Did you notify the police?"

"I'm doing that next, but first I wanted you to know. These pieces are under contract. You'll have to help make this right."

The underpinnings of normalcy had collapsed. Merle felt gelatinous, melting in molten heat. He fanned himself and gazed at a faded watercolor of a Bavarian snow scene. "Call the cops. I can get there by noon." His angst recalibrated toward the nimrods responsible for the deviant act.

An hour later, hungry for a heavy, comforting lunch, Merle wobbled at the carnage before him, parts decoupled as if a gang of chimpanzees had raided with wrenches. The profuse scale of the vandalism merged with the extant, esoteric land slipping from his grasp. Trees bobbed in a derisive breeze, his acumen scorned and unwanted. He would call the partners and insurance company, and focus energy on exit strategies. "Mannequin" must mean "cursed," he surmised, but someone would suffer for this latest salvo.

He would make sure of it.

56

A cookpot clanked against the frame of Reily's backpack, signaling his and Wil's approach, if anyone cared or listened. Night advanced on the endurance march to a makeshift campsite at the far end of the watershed. The forest loomed extra spacious, an earthly galaxy for revelry on the emancipating cusp of summer.

A cone of light from a motorcycle wove between trees, carrying the tremolo of a wounded bee. Reily breathed Eddie's exhaust. Marlin bristled at the dissonance. Motorized transport violated an inherent law of campouts—labor sweetened the experience.

Eddie rolled up to them, helmetless, and cut the motor. "Boom, Cindy, and Rachel are already back there. You two Jethros better hurry up." He had a crazy face, enflamed by liberty and testosterone.

"We're carrying all the food, lazy ass." Reily readjusted his sagging load. "I thought you cracked the block on that thing?"

Eddie reflexively scanned the shadows of his engine. "No, it just needed a spark plug."

Wil cracked up. He wore a baseball hat backwards, a new style for him . . . teenage Oscar Madison.

"You let it sit for a year because you didn't check the plug?" Eddie showed initiative only when it came to painting. Other efforts were on whim, however infrequently they struck.

Marlin whimpered. Reily patted his side. "Time's a-wasting, gentlemen. Let's move out, but don't go tearing up the woods, Evel Knievel."

Eddie answered with an obscene gesture.

Two tents stood at the site, one a larger, triangular, bile green version of the other. Wil's tent, diminutive by comparison, came in deer hunter orange. Reily helped set it up, ten yards beyond the others. Sleeping assignments were predetermined, but not discussed. He feared grotesque lip-to-lip auditory from his sister and Eddie, or that Wil might squeeze him while dreaming of the Kelly that got away. Mostly, he wished his own former prize catch would someday return.

Boom contained more excitement than a fawn learning to walk. "We must make the fire bigger."

Eddie tossed handfuls of sticks and hefty limbs onto smoldering coals until a sporting event could have taken place in the middle of the wilds.

The "ground star of Bethlehem," as Reily tagged the inferno, illuminated their short-term settlement and encouraged them to wander. Above, a releafed canopy of scrawny maples and good-sized walnuts veiled them from the outer world. Below, fallen leaves decayed on schedule, deadening their voices. Boom and Cindy examined a maple sapling top to bottom, like a physician and dentist working over the same patient. The plant doctors consulted.

"I believe it is a sugar maple." Boom managed to reign in his volume, in accordance with forest ethics.

"Definitely not." Cindy could be assertive without raising her voice. She tugged Boom to his knees. "See the vertical lines on the bark."

"Yes, yes. I see."

"Striped maple. Now you know. Don't forget." She pinched his side. "It's a successional species . . . I learned that from Mr. Kreider. This looks like a young forest, probably cleared in recent years." Cindy gazed around, evaluating. "We can't be far from the quarry." The happy botanical couple blended into the shadows. Reily wondered what lay beyond.

Closer to the light, Eddie fed Rachel contents of a bottle, babbling and bickering to one another, inches apart. Rachel asserted that women would soon occupy most seats of government, from county courthouses to the White House. "We're the superior sex," she said. "Get used to it, Edward." Wil must have slipped away, likely not far, to escape their jousting and glean nocturnal insights in the great outside. Reily inhaled the lusty exhalations of their forest and sat against a wrinkled trunk, basking in the juices of the present. Marlin lay at his side, content and dreaming, twitching from an imagined chase.

Somber drops of rain quashed the quietude, first tempering, then dismantling the unseasonable heat. The atmosphere roared. Bodies sought refuge.

Cocooned in the tent, Reily used a spare shirt to wipe Marlin's fur. The thump of footsteps forewarned Wil's return before he dove inside, prewashing their belongings with his drippings.

Wil struggled to catch his breath. "There's equipment out there."

Reily passed him the shirt in a useless attempt to keep stuff dry. "What are you talking about?" Marlin cocked his head, equally confused.

"Big stuff. Bulldozers. Tree removers."

"Tree removers?"

Wil shrugged. "I don't know what they're called. They have mandibles."

"They are kind of like jaws, Marlin, but don't worry, they won't come after us."

"We have to do something." Wil shook his head, sprinkling the interior. "Come with me."

"Right now?"

"If you don't come, I'm peeing in here."

"But it's your tent . . ."

"Good point."

"Marlin, you stay here, boy. Only one of us needs to get soaked."

Reily had nothing waterproof except a balled up windbreaker, squished in the bottom of the pack. He slipped it on, zipped Marlin inside the A-frame, and followed Wil—two flashlights bobbing through the rainforest.

Wil's beam stabbed a pack of school bus yellow, mechanical monsters, dripping and asleep. Reily crept closer to inspect. Tracks in a cleared void suggested more equipment had come and gone, but the pieces present contained plenty of destructive power. Some had parts separated or missing—bolts on the ground, a tire absent on a front-end loader.

Either a repairperson had taken an extended break, or someone less supportive had tinkered with the Tonka toys.

Merle rolled around on his Broyhill sofa like a hot dog on a grill, tonged by vandals cooking away his fortunes. Television transmitted little solace. With machines still on site, the hoodlums might be back for more demolition. He would be there . . . *to make them forever afraid of the Darkes.*

Merle loaded a shotgun with 20-gauge birdshot and placed it on the rear floor of the Jeep. In his one and only use of the gun, he missed every clay pigeon in a skeet event hosted by an investors group. The gleaming barrel and polished stock exemplified defiance, a lethal symbol sure to deter thieves and thugs.

The tiresome drivel of windshield wipers became a hypnotic metronome on Merle's anger-driven drive. His mother, now absent auditory stimuli, despised noise of any type. She'd rescinded his xylophone at his fifth birthday party, after sending home the only guest for emptying a wastebasket on the floor and using it is as a drum. In contrast, there were better, more motherly moments, like when he trenched a pretend river on an adjoining property. The neighbor became furious. Mom professed dislike for the old codger and Merle benefitted with an extra slice of pie for dessert. Mom certainly loved her pie.

But he wanted the bigger pie, the one baking for over a year and burned by bureaucrats. Local meddlers chomped on the crumbs, hastening his forthcoming famine. They would have to pay for their meal.

Merle crawled in low gear up the drowning access road, headlights revealing sludgy rivulets oozing downhill. Short of the staging area–turned–equipment evacuation zone, he parked in spongy darkness, zipped his waterproof slicker, and retrieved a flashlight from the glovebox. He closed the car door with nary a sound.

At the back of the car, he hauled out the Browning, absorbing temporary comfort from its weight.

The rain lightened but held steady—a clammy, dreary shower. Merle's eyes adjusted to the miniscule light rebounding from scudding clouds. The impermanent clearing made him feel naked, vulnerable. *What if the bad guys have a gun?* Nervousness mutated to self-pity. *No sane person would be out here moping about.* If he had a *real* life, he would be snug in bed, with a steamy companion of the opposite sex.

Sudden mumblings, faint but definitive, escaped the forest, accompanied by erratic beads of light. He crouched low and watched. Silhouettes snuck beneath the hulk of machines bored from inactivity. One of the cretins climbed up on an operator's seat and jiggled a lever. Merle boiled within. He lifted the shotgun and advanced—one silent step at a time.

57

"What are you doing up there?" Reily spoke in a harsh whisper, worried about imagined would-be listeners.

Wil groped at the controls of one of the man-made dinosaurs. "Trying to find a key."

"They wouldn't leave them out here. Come on down, there's nothing we can do tonight to save the woods."

Flash. The universe exploded. Wil tumbled. Reily scattered. A second deafening barrage. Reily raced, dodging trees, speculating at sonic speed as to the source of the bombardment. A volley of livid shouts trailed him. He skidded under a patch of mountain laurel and contrived death, immobile as a mummy, resting upon wet earth. No sign of firelight, but the hollering returned, louder and maniacal, cursing in the brush. *Keep moving.* Reily scrambled to his feet and plowed forward. A limb gouged his shoulder. Fear anesthetized pain. Nothing in the limited field of vision seemed familiar. *Where are the others? Where is Wil?*

A harsh snap echoed on the right. He bolted all out through another fortress of laurel, for a microsecond questioning the strange, straightedge termination of forest. Reily plummeted, lamenting the absence of solid ground beneath his feet. He braced for an uncontrolled splashdown fearing instantaneous death.

From a prone position, Wil crawled in the direction of a muffled, but unmistakable plop. He came upon the lip of the local Grand Canyon and cupped his ears, struggling to hear more than his thumping pulse.

Except for the irregular freefall of droplets from leaves, the forest grew muted in the wake of the rain—the yelling and footsteps gone, or at least unheard.

From below, a swirl. The slow churn of a tired swimmer. Wil opened his mouth to speak, but abstained. *Shotgun pyscho might be lurking*.

Concern superseded fright. "Who's down there?" Wil directed his appeal at the nothingness with a bellow barely audible.

The quarry repeated the words.

He waited, the silence chilling like saturated clothes.

Again, he called.

"Wil, is that you?" A recognizable accent, but meagre and distant.

"Yeah, it's me. What happened?"

"What do you think?"

Wil suppressed a laugh. "Are you okay?"

"I hurt my arm. I'm standing on a ledge, but the water is really cold." Worry filled Reily's voice.

"Stay put. I'll be back."

"Where do you think I'm going?"

After a punishing ramble, Wil found a clump of four bodies—refugees from combat—amassed between familiar portable dwellings. Rachel had Marlin on a leash.

"What the hell happened?" Eddie looked crazed.

With haste, Wil reconstructed the sequence of events. "Reily opted for a swim. We have to get him out of the pit."

Cindy, shell-shocked, stared into the beyond. "Are you sure it's safe?"

Rachel clicked on her flashlight. "It doesn't matter. My brother needs help."

"Hold on a second." Wil jogged to his tent, recovered the trusted topo map, and returned to his distressed friends. "Okay, let's go." He motioned them to keep quiet and follow. The rescue team departed. Danger had a way of making everyone compliant.

Wil chastened the leaves. Even wet, they blathered when agitated. He sensed the terrain hardening, quarry leftovers underfoot. "We're almost there. Watch your step."

They stopped at the precipice. Marlin whined.

"Wil? Marlin?" Reily sounded adrift.

Marlin whined again, and disassociated from Rachel. She reached. He sprang. Wil beheld his first flying dog.

With a gasp, they waited for impact. *Kersploosh.*

"What was that?" Reily squeaked the question likely knowing the answer.

"Marlin," Boom volunteered, with too much volume.

Reily called to Marlin, rapt with urgency.

They waited with held breath, choking on silence.

Another despondent plea from Reily.

A faint, rhythmic pulse. Subtle at first, then unmistakable.

A long minute later, a garbled message verified a reunion in the hole. Wil worried about the cold water. "How can we get them out of there?"

He dropped to his knees and opened the map. Cindy shined a light on it. The contour lines revealed a lower spot and lesser slope in the northeast corner. The north side seemed the shortest route, but the land rose sharply facing the quarry, and dropped away on the backside toward the valley. It would have to do. Watters and the dog would need to take another swim to reach the corner, assuming it offered a way out.

Say of the Day: dire.

Operation Reily Recovery initiated. Cindy and Boom escorted Wil as they made for the extraction point. Eddie and Rachel went to retrieve the motorcycle and any and all pieces of rope from the encampment.

With each step, loose rocks shifted as Wil scrambled across the dumped overburden pitched at forty-five degrees. Boom skied away, but caught a rusted signpost, intended to keep kids *out* of danger. Indiscriminate trees poked through the rubble, adamant about living. Wil hoped Reily and Marlin had the same determination. Eighth grade health class had spelled out the risks of hypothermia, including the prospect of death. The slow slog had already sucked away ten precious minutes.

Wil clambered ahead on an awkward slant, making for the juncture. An abrupt corner came into view. The moonscape lowered. Foreboding water hid twenty feet below. The wall remained steep, but had a crack wide enough to stand in halfway down.

"I think this will work." Wil shimmied, foot by foot, for the crevasse. Once positioned, he called up to Boom and Cindy. "I'll need your help pulling."

A giant insect plied the forest, gaining on them. "I hear Eddie's motorcycle." Boom's decree evoked needed hope in the throes of their crisis.

"Reily," Wil bellowed, caution cast aside. "Swim this way . . . bring Marlin, too." The statement seemed ridiculous as soon as he said it. Marlin wasn't a toy poodle you could stuff under an arm. Who knew if dog or owner had the mobility or energy to cover the distance.

"I'm freezing," Reily broadcasted back to him.

"No excuses, Watters."

Motorcycle madman Eddie buzzed nearby. Cindy summoned him with her flashlight.

Eddie and Rachel dismounted. He twirled a section of skinny rope. "That was a wild ride."

Rachel glared at Wil through the dimness, as if everything was his fault. "Eddie almost killed me. Anyway, we found clothesline in your pack and tied on tent cords. If we double it up, it should hold weight, but it isn't very long."

Wil gauged the distance to the surface. Ten feet would suffice. The vertical rock face angled slightly.

Out of the gloom, two bizarre shadows rippled the eerie lake. "C'mon boy." A sidestroking Reily nudged Marlin along.

Wil directed them his way. "Just a few more yards." Eddie slid into position beside him and dislodged a thin slab of slate.

Marlin arrived first and attempted to ascend. Dog nails were no match for smooth rock. Marlin flailed. Eddie turned lifeguard.

Coordination occurred without words. Boom stole Eddie's spot adjoining Wil and picked up the rope, letting it uncoil. "Eddie, take it and push Marlin upwards."

The first try failed, but on the second attempt, Marlin cooperated. Eddie nudged his back end. A tiny bit of traction and a big shove by Eddie cantilevered Marlin on to the perch. Boom helped the dog the rest of the way to the top.

Removing Reily would be another matter. One of Reily's arms didn't seem to be working, and Eddie had little to brace against for advantage when pushing.

Wil gripped his end of the jerry-rigged rope and nodded for Boom to assist. "Hold on tight with your left hand, Reily. One way or another, we're going to pull you up."

They heaved. Reily strained. Eddie flattened himself against the rock. Onlookers might assume he had an abnormal passion for geology. The weird position gave Reily a temporary foothold. Eddie wormed for higher ground. Reily ascended and winced in pain, one arm held close to his body.

Safe on the upper rim, Reily shivered like an earthquake. Rachel helped place him on to the back of Eddie's idling motorbike. "Hold on with your good arm."

Cindy—the unflappable doctor—draped her jacket around the injured. "This might help."

Reily groaned. "Let it be known, I'm no longer afraid of heights." The words came out jumbled from a numb face.

Boom tapped Reily's shoulder. Reily acknowledged him with a glazed, goofy leer.

"Your dog deserves a new name."

"Huh?"

"He shall now be known as *Blue* Marlin." The declaration pierced the engine noise.

"Ah . . . as in water," Reily slurred. "The Blue Marlin wins the *day*."

"Ha, exactly, and helped save your life."

Reily asked for his dog. Marlin approached the stinky cycle, limping slightly. "You're a brave pup." Reily rubbed Marlin's ear with his better hand. "Stay here. I'll see you soon."

Eddie revved the bike and pulled away.

Rachel called after them, "Take him straight to the emergency room."

Wil paraded the remaining crew back to the campsite via the longer, but more level, southern route. A breeze arose, the clouds fell apart. Stars broke out like beacons leading them home.

They dismantled and stowed gear with apathy in the darkness. When the belongings were ready for transport, Wil remobilized the disheveled unit. "We're going out on the road."

Rachel spat as they passed the big equipment. Boom cursed in Swahili. Cindy used her flashlight, searching for something.

She halted. "Wil, did you say the blasts came from this direction?"

"Definitely. We were here when it started."

"Well, have a look at this." Cindy knelt to the ground and stood up with a shotgun shell, the casing unblemished. "Forensic evidence, I do believe."

Rachel displayed her most caustic scowl. "Some chickenshit ran away after playing with their gun."

Wil regarded the spent ammo in Cindy's hand, putting together the mental pieces for a future story . . . a most harrowing and award-winning adolescent tale.

58

Reily's sling invited pity, questions, and umpteen requests to retell the traumatic saga. Word spread about his injury and after school, on the last day, he detected a sheepish tap upon his front door and opened it. Colleen Mills stood before him, putting an exclamation point on the end of the academic year.

An apology by Colleen led to an embrace and subsequent face-to-face interaction. The sequence, and her irresistible presence, relegated last shreds of torn feelings to interstellar dust. Who could have guessed that a standard medical device had the power to reconstitute desire?

That night, at the courts, Reily aced one-armed shots while receiving Wil's oral dissertation on the psychology of Ms. Kelly Bingham, *his* reinstated duchess of desire. The subject deserved multiple hypotheses, but one surpassed all others: experiencing extended deprivation of attention, she reverted to the simplest recourse—baiting weak and defenseless Wil Wisnoski for short-term kicks.

"So be it," Wil said. "I'll let her have her fun."

"She called you before the campout and you didn't tell me?"

"After she reached out, I had a king-sized plan—a midnight rendez-vous in mind—but she had to go away that weekend." Wil squeezed a basketball between his hands. "I didn't want to talk about it."

Reily wanted to laugh at Wil. He had the Oscar Madison look again, with brown hair winging sideways below the reversed cap. "You're such a sucker."

"Yeah, well, you're a fallfish."

Reily threw a ball at Wil, but it missed, hitting the chain link fence with a familiar *ching*. "We're both pathetic."

"Yes, but our pathos will lead to eros." Wil's hazy blue peepers glowed mystically.

"Where do you get these words? I thought I was Secretary of Philosophy."

"Always, but I am the Deacon of Love." Wil clutched his heart for emphasis. "And my parents are going away this very Friday."

"Without you . . . again?" Wil's parents left him alone so often, he might as well have had his own apartment.

"It's their anniversary. First stop is a car show in Carlisle, and then a night in Greenbrier, West Virginia. I told them you would stay over. They trust *you*."

"Are you suggesting what I think you're suggesting?"

"We'll give the ladies the night of their lives."

On two wheels, steering with his functioning arm, Reily transported a written invitation, scribbled on notebook paper, to Miss Colleen Mills. Wil used the telephone to inquire with Kelly Bingham. Both methods brought desired results.

With a lineup informed by the dietary routines of the carnivorous Watters family, the dinner menu consisted of grilled sirloin steaks, baked potatoes, and a tossed salad with Green Goddess dressing. Reily shopped alone Thursday evening, hiding the undercover groceries in the basement refrigerator seldom used. While plugging in the backup appliance, he crawled beneath the dusty countertop anchored to the wall where his father tinkered on home repair projects. In the dull light, Reily touched tools—a wrench, crowbar, and massive screwdriver—crusted with dirt and leaves.

At Wil's, he told of the discovery.

Wil nodded matter-of-factly. "What a coincidence. My dad left a pile of extra-large tools in need of washing in the corner of the garage."

"Does this mean our Dads are—"

"Badass? Yes, it does. Environmental guerillas like those Greenpeace people."

Reily felt his jaw agape. "This changes everything."

"Not really, same old pops. Now we know how much they care about this stuff. But it doesn't matter."

"What do you mean?"

"You didn't hear? The government, as in the American government, won't let them build the dam. They nixed it."

"Really?" Reily brimmed with relief. Visions of Mannequin Creek National Park danced in his delighted head.

"Yep, it's official, but we can't dwell on it. We have arrangements to make."

"Excuse me?"

Wil tossed him a black t-shirt. "Put this on. We're going on an adventure."

The mission landed them next door. Reily found himself crawling on the ground beside Wil, the thick lawn giving off a pure, fresh smell he wished he could bottle and use as cologne for the rest of the year. Wil stopped beneath underclothes overhead. His neighbor forgot to take them off the line.

"What are we doing?" Reily whispered.

"She has amazing blossoms."

"You're such a Peeping Tom."

"I'm talking about hydrangeas." Wil faked dismay, and smiled like a rapscallion. "I like her roses, too."

"We're going to steal her flowers?"

"Borrow them, like Eddie would."

At 6:32 P.M. on Friday evening, an hour after Mr. and Mrs. Wisnoski's departure, Colleen eyed Reily with a promising pose at Wil's front door. With pulled back onyx hair, she smoldered in a frilly top and jeans, snug and superb. Five minutes later, Kelly parked her mother's car along the curb, at the end of the front walkway. She wore white bell-bottoms, and a low-cut indigo blouse, with eye shadow to match. The girls were utterly stunning, or, as Wil might say, top-notch. They even liked the flowers. The respective bouquets fell short of florist standards, but the mere gesture mattered most.

Wil grilled, splashing on sauces and seasonings like a professional. Reily turned head waiter, attending to the dining table, pouring sparkling grape juice into long-stemmed glasses, and turning up the live 8-track of

Peter Frampton on the portable player. He noticed Colleen grooving to the tunes, shoulders swaying, waiting.

Dinner impressed, although Wil splattered sour cream on Kelly's cleavage. The carbonation of the faux fancy wine caused Reily to burp inadvertently. A fly disrupted free-flowing conversation, dually attracted by the aroma of steaks and yard flowers, but Reily didn't care and neither did the others. The night superseded all norms and expectations.

Reily washed the dishes shuttled into the sink by the girls. A sinking sun mellowed the interior light. Wil changed the music to the sappy, soothing vocals of a band called Bread and moved the player to the living room. With cleanup completed to temporary standards, Reily summoned the girls to the romance zone. He and Colleen squeezed into one end of the boat-like sofa. Kelly and Wil took the port side. Four small glasses, filled in equal minor amounts, contained an amber liquid—samples from Mr. Wisnoski's special occasion cognac collection. It *required* drinking, despite the risk, for the moments surely shattered the standard for special.

Upon the next album, the couples adjourned to respective private quarters. Wil increased the volume until rock and roll permeated the house. Reily slid open the window in the Wisnoski guest room, overheated by the weather, the companion, or both. Colleen wrapped her arms around him. She smelled better than the perfume aisle at Wanamaker's. Much better than any grass-made aftershave.

They lowered themselves to the edge of the bed, Colleen pressed against his side. "I think I'm going to play field hockey next year," she said, with an air of self-confidence previously unseen. "Maybe goalie . . . since I'm so good at getting in the way of things." She peered upwards, seeking forgiveness. "I need focus, and exercise. Plus, Mallory has a terrible team. They can use all the help they can get."

Reily locked an arm around her. "I better learn more about field hockey." He remembered the surprise in his pocket, and stood to get it out. "I have something for you." He handed her a piece of folded, lined paper. "It's a poem I wrote a while ago."

Colleen held it for an excruciating moment. "I can't wait to read it." She set it aside and sprang into his arms, initiating another kiss. This one tasted as good as all the others, but lingered on.

Slowly, the Wisnoski home grew dark and inaudible, except for the spirited pronouncements of Mick Jagger and the Stones . . . rambling toward midnight with get-what-you-need satisfaction.

59

Wil walked backward, appraising his three friends. "I can't believe they're graduates. Cindy and Rachel forever freed from classroom bells and morning announcements."

Boom beamed, brighter than normal. "My parents gave Cindy fifty dollars."

Eddie shrugged. "I gave Rachel ten bucks."

Reily put Eddie in a good-humored headlock with his one arm that worked. "It's the thought that matters."

The misfits made a sorry sight, but Wil would never swap them. "Sorry I missed the ceremony. Mom needed help with an order for a wedding reception. I had to decorate two hundred iced cookies."

Frumpy Eddie looked him up and down. "Did you bring any extras?"

"None for you."

Boom dimmed. "Cindy leaves for college at the end of the month. I know we may not remain boyfriend and girlfriend, but I hope we stay friends." His version of melancholy had solace. The light still shined, at least inwardly.

Eyes went to Eddie—the other guy with a departing gal. "What? Rachel doesn't go to Dickinson until August." He munched on his lower lip, a sure sign of fretting. "I realized she never asked me to the prom . . . not that I'm much into that kind of thing."

Reily slapped his own forehead in jest. "Only seniors can go to the prom, brick brain."

Eddie had ample reason to wallow. Things between the kooky couple were headed downhill. A Connecticut boy Rachel had once met on a ski club trip to the Catskills also had a ticket to Dickinson College. They had become pen pals for a second time. Thanks to Reily, Wil had read the tempting correspondence.

Wil stopped at a new "for sale" sign in front of the Kemps' former driveway. He looked at Reily. "This is nice to see."

"I suppose," Reily grunted as he viewed the desolation, now sprouting rebelliously. "I despise destruction for no good reason."

The solstice would transpire in two weeks, but summer did not wait for this crew. Away from the Kemp Farm ruins, the woods were festive this Sunday morning. Wil became an organism of the earth as he hiked, smiling to no one in particular. A hawk screamed from a treetop. Eddie screeched back. The mountain laurel robed itself in white blossoms with a splash of pink. Bees flourished with nectar-sipping, pollen-hauling maneuvers. A squirrel excavated with ursine tendencies.

Say of the Day: fecundity.

Boom regaled them with breaking news from Cindy. "Her father is a Deputy District Attorney, and he told her that the man that chased us—"

"You mean shot at us." Reily snapped his fingers at Marlin to distract him from eating deer droppings.

"Yes, shot at us . . . he has been charged with reckless endangerment." Boom pronounced the term like a seasoned lawyer.

"Sounds nice and harsh." Eddie flicked a booger from his finger. "How did they figure out that dam builder dude did it?"

"Cindy." When Boom said her name, his face seemed to celebrate. "The ammunition she found matched a gun found in the front seat of Mr. Darkes's car when he was pulled over for a broken taillight the night of the crime. He must have been so worried about what he had done, he backed into a tree when he left the forest. The law he broke is a second-degree misdemeanor. He could be fined or go to prison. Cindy also told me that they could make him donate to an environmental charity."

"Excellent. They should make him do reforestation—for life." Reily carried his grandpa's duffel over the shoulder. The canvas had worn out from too many expeditions. He had told Wil with a dejected expression that this would be its last circuit, its final spree. "Speaking of excellent, did I tell you about my English grade?"

"What a dweeb." Eddie puffed his chest and pushed a hand into an undersized glove. "This is where Jethro and I leave you two scholastic freaks. We have snakes to catch."

Boom fingered the camera hanging from his neck. "We're seeking copperheads on the east side of the quarry. Mr. Kreider believes it could be a denning site."

"Please don't harass the snakes, gentlemen." Reily spoke with calm authority. Jesus of the Mannequin.

Wil watched Boom and Eddie plod away. "You heard the arbiter of the wilderness. He has spoken. We'll be at the loch. And don't get bitten. One forest rescue is enough." Wil turned to his oldest friend. "We better get moving. There are fish to catch."

He squeezed past branches on the creekside path, striving to avoid a tangled ball of fishing line. "Did I tell you I signed up for a writing camp at Middlebury College?"

Reily hummed as he ambled forward, lost in thought with Marlin as his wingman. "No, that's cool. Where's Middlebury?"

"Vermont. In the Green Mountains."

"Steve Patterson invited me to go canoeing in the Boundary Waters of Minnesota the first week in August. You should go, too."

"Can't do. That's family vacation week." Wil felt a rush of cool air that signified the proximate, tempting, neutralizing magnificence of water. Maybe the graduations had inflicted a bite of nostalgia, but at that moment Wil felt what Reily sometimes lamented: the transient glory of runaway days. "I should have told you this a week ago . . . I talked to Coach Finn. I'm going to swim next year."

"Outstanding," Reily mumbled. Hair obscured his face. Reily's hair grew faster than dandelions.

Marlin roamed off-leash, a docile wolf on ancestral lands. The watershed called to him like it did to his master, emollient to the mad world beyond. The immortal pool known as the loch came into view, resting before them as transcendent as Edward Knisely's prize-winning watercolor. "We are destined for lake-ness, my friend."

Lochside, Reily positioned a radio pulled from the duffel and searched for the best station. Upon fine-tuning, "Reeling in the Years" played without static. "That's more like it," Wil said as he prepped his best guess, fish-fooling apparatus.

Reily leaned against the tree Eddie had depicted. Marlin laid flat on the big rock, respiring with gladness, attuned to any possibility. Wil flipped his line into the realm where minutes blurred into hours.

After an unknown lapse of time and uncounted casts, Wil planned to switch to a different lure, but a tug-of-war commenced, more intense than most. A creature left the water and reentered, preparing for the summer Olympics. A second launch reached new heights, bending the light. Five minutes of struggle and aerobatics ended in submission.

Apparition no more, Wil coddled a twelve-inch, record brook trout. Marlin administered a sniff test.

Reily stared, pleased. "That's the biggest brook I've ever seen."

"Top-notch." Wil kneeled beside the hallowed catch. "I may have to keep this one. No one will believe me if I don't."

"I will. I'm the witness." Reily stepped to the rock beside the pool. "Let it go. Something so perfect can never be taken."

Ode to Streams

A Poem by Reily Watters

Sunrays lap the leaves
Leaves that leave us whole
That laugh along and listen
Lifting spirits with their dew
Stewing love and desire
For adventure oft inspired
Aspire along the water
To make a perfect day

About the Author

Brook Lenker is a passionate conservationist, explorer, and author of the 2019 novel, *The Restorers*. He served as a contributing writer for *After the Pandemic: Visions of Life Post COVID-19*, a nonfiction volume, and freelanced for Susquehanna Life Magazine for nearly a decade. Infused by a love of nature and adventures near and far, his writings evoke memorable characters and rich depictions of place that stir readers. A graduate of Towson University with degrees in Geography, Brook is the proud father of two adult daughters. He lives along the Yellow Breeches Creek in South Central Pennsylvania with his wife and a collie named Zena.